Damon's voice held me spellbound.
I might just be...
aft...

His warm breath blew against my chilled flesh. I went on alert, stiffening.

"What are you doing?" I asked.

"Trying to get you to relax."

A feather-soft kiss seared my skin.

"Stop it, Damon."

His hands were on my nape again, kneading, soothing.

"You're wound as tight as a spring."

I hated to admit it, but Damon's massaging hands on my back felt wonderful. My entire body was beginning to tingle and buzz.

"Take off your clothes."

"What?"

"You heard me."

Books by Marcia King-Gamble

MARCIA KING-GAMBLE

is a national bestselling author and a former travel industry executive. She's lived in five different states and has traveled to some of the most exotic parts of the world. The Far East, Venice, Italy, and New Zealand are still her favorites.

She enjoys a good workout, and is passionate about animals, old houses and tearjerker movies. Marcia is also the editor of a monthly newsletter entitled *Marcia's Romantically Yours.* Log on to her Web site, www.lovemarcia.com, and find out what she's all about.

MARCIA KING-GAMBLE

MEET PHOENIX

KIMANI™
ROMANCE

"As you read may you find your own Divine Wisdom."

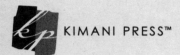

KIMANI PRESS™

ISBN-13: 978-0-373-86077-7
ISBN-10:   0-373-86077-3

MEET PHOENIX

Copyright © 2008 by Marcia King-Gamble

Dear Reader,

I have been fortunate enough to spend some time in the Far East, and love it. Each visit is treasured and each time I return to the United States I feel more enriched. At one point in my life I even considered moving there. When that did not materialize, I satisfied my yearnings for places like Hong Kong, Singapore and Bangkok by taking frequent trips.

Even now the old architecture, mysticism and spiritualism of Asia continue to draw me. Combine those with elegant dining, endless hours of shopping and visits to mosques and temples, and I'm in my own state of nirvana.

Needless to say, when I got the opportunity to write an action-adventure story set in Tibet, I was really excited. Tibet is one of the few places I haven't visited, and I had to rely on research. After immersing myself in the culture, Tibet is now one of my top ten places to visit.

Buddhism is also a religion that has interested me. Maybe it has something to do with having an enormous crush on Richard Gere, who runs neck and neck with Denzel Washington as the two sexiest men on the planet. Or maybe my high energy requires that calming effect.

What I do know is I created my hero, Damon Hernandez, with Denzel's smile and Richard's sexy walk in mind. Let me know if I was successful in creating a to-die-for hero and a strong, sensual heroine.

If you've enjoyed reading *Meet Phoenix,* I'd love to know. Please drop me an e-mail at mkinggambl@aol.com, or write me at P.O. Box 25143, Fort Lauderdale, Florida. And if you want to know what I'm up to, visit me frequently at www.lovemarcia.com. I'm always off on one adventure or another.

Happy travels,

Marcia King-Gamble

Chapter 1

"I will not allow you to commit him." I tightly clutched the phone and swiveled around in my office chair.

"There may be no other choice," my aunt Estelle said. "Since yesterday he's been almost catatonic."

My eyes burned and tension weighed between my shoulder blades. This was my father she was talking about. I knew he had problems but to commit him to a psychiatric institution? Unthinkable.

I knew he was depressed, but the only therapeutic shock treatment Thomas Sutherland needed was to have his name cleared. And I intended to do just that. It was one of the reasons I'd accepted this assignment in Tibet.

Aunt Estelle was going on and on about how debilitating depression was. I blinked the moisture from my eyes, stuck my head out of the open studio window and focused on the leaves pooling around the trees. Taxis whizzed by. The sky was a cloudless, brilliant blue. Fall in New York promised to be beautiful.

"Can we discuss this later?" I said softly and hung up. I just couldn't deal with this today. Plus, they couldn't commit him without my consent anyway.

"Althea's on the other line," Whitley Montgomery, my assistant, called from the outer room.

I took a deep breath of the brisk morning air and picked up the receiver. Althea Wright and I had met eight years ago at an art institute in Florence, Italy. I was in the conservation program, devoted to the preservation of cultural heritage, and Althea was in the restoration program, which restores and reconstructs the work of art back to its "original" state. Or at least close to it. Ever since then we were as tight as two people could be.

"Hey, you caught me at the right time, Althea."

I injected gaiety into my voice. I welcomed any distraction.

"Is that Tibetan trip still on? You did say you needed someone with expertise in reconstruction."

"Does that mean what I think it does?"

"Yup. I'm coming if you'll still have me."

I needed this news. I could use both my best friend's expertise *and* her support.

"Of course I'll have you, silly girl. We're about to make history. We'll be working on a statue that is as important as the Messiah is to the Western world. Maitreya's finding is heralded like the second coming of Christ. He's considered the universal teacher."

"Yes, I know. He's one of three priceless Buddhas crafted by an artisan back in 500 B.C. How long will we be gone?"

"At the very least, three months."

"Three months, Phoenix? That's more than enough time for you to get into your usual trouble. And it's a long time for both of us to be away from our studios. The Tibetan government had better be paying us well."

I named a figure then went on to say, "If we meet the deadline we get a bonus. There just aren't any artisans in Tibet qualified to reconstruct a piece this rare."

This was exactly the kind of project I loved. I'd read and reread every article I could get my hands on about this rare finding. Even now a newspaper lay on my desk, the headline prominently displayed.

Maitreya, Future Buddha Found By Gardener.

Something wasn't quite right though. It was definitely odd that all of a sudden a missing Buddha would show up in a *garden,* of all places. Plus, if my suspicions were confirmed, it would be an opportunity to clear my father's name.

Whitley rapped on the door and stuck her head in through the crack, signaling time-out.

"Got to go, Althea," I said, hanging up the phone and waving Whit in.

"Some guy's outside asking to see you."

"I don't remember making an appointment."

"You probably didn't write it down. Stop picking up your own calls and we wouldn't have these issues. What should I do with him?" Whit asked.

I rose to my full height of five feet nine inches and rested my butt against the desk, crossing one denim-clad leg over the other. "Does *him* have a name?"

"Yup. Him has a card, too." Whit flipped a business card in my direction. "Him is a hottie."

I glanced at the crisp white card and my breath hitched.

What did Damon Hernandez want? It had been eight years since I'd last laid eyes on him.

"Send him in," I said, curiosity getting the better of me.

"I'm already in," a deep male voice said from the doorway, the Bronx accent very pronounced.

My heart palpitated and then settled, but my stomach was a different story. Must be the fried chicken and chips from lunch… I fumbled, found the Tums I kept in the pocket of my shirt, and quickly popped one.

The last I'd heard, Damon Hernandez was still in Europe, and that had been just fine with me.

"Heartburn, Phe? Tell me life isn't that rough."

I managed a smile. I would not let his appearance rattle me. I would not let those dark good looks, tight curls and dreamy gray eyes fog up my thinking. No trips down memory lane. That would not be permitted.

"How are you, Damon?" I asked. "And to what do I owe this pleasure?"

"Doing well, Phe. I was in the neighborhood and thought I'd swing by and take you out for coffee."

I hiked an eyebrow. "It's been a long time."

Silence. We just stared at each other.

"Cut the bull, Damon. Why are you here?"

"I've missed you, Phe," he said, taking a step

closer. "Missed that lovely face of yours, those wonderfully sculpted cheekbones and sparkling eyes."

I stepped back and swept a lock of straightened brown hair off my cheek. I considered popping another Tums since the one I'd downed seconds ago was lodged in my chest. *Why had I chosen today of all days to wear baggy overalls?*

Whit was openly following the conversation. I could almost hear her brain clicking, trying to figure out how we knew each other. With a slight movement of my head, I dismissed her. To him I gestured to the most uncomfortable chair in the cramped office.

"Damon," I said, "I don't have time for coffee today. Grab a seat."

He flopped into the chair and I retreated behind the safety of my desk.

Breathe, dammit! Breathe! Don't let him see how much he rattles you. What you two had is long over with.

"Ah, Phe, you haven't changed at all," Damon continued, his gaze sliding over me. "If anything, you're lovelier than ever."

He must want something. I stuffed both hands into the pockets of my denim overalls and waited.

"Suppose you tell me why you're really here?" I asked, reasoning that my heated cheeks had to do more with his irksome presence than irrepressible hormones.

"Phe, you suspicious woman." Damon chuckled, a deep-throated sound. "I came to see you, and find out how your dad's doing?"

My dad was a sensitive topic.

I was protective of the father who'd raised me and four brothers single-handedly, since my mom died when I was five. Dad, once a museum curator in Asian art, was brilliant but eccentric. I loved him with utter devotion. He'd encouraged me to pursue a career in art conservation and restoration and we'd dreamt of one day working together.

I still held on to that dream.

"Holding his own," I answered, not elaborating.

"That's good. Must have been tough losing that job."

"Very tough."

Damon didn't have to know how badly Dad's condition had deteriorated after he'd been fired, and how a paralyzing depression had set in.

"So is your father the reason you've accepted an assignment in Tibet?" Damon held a hand up, preventing me from cutting him off. "I heard about the trip via the grapevine. You're going because you hope to clear your dad's name?"

I blinked at Damon but kept my tone even. "There's nothing to clear. My father is innocent."

"I know that," Damon said in the tone that used to give me goose bumps. *Used to,* being the operative words. "But you'll be needing an experienced X-ray infrared technologist along, yes? I'm at your service."

So that was why he was here. Word had gotten out that I'd been awarded the coveted assignment of preserving the Maitreya. Damon, self-serving as always, was here to capitalize on my good luck.

"I'll interview one if I need one," I countered.

Damon catapulted out of his chair, approaching my desk. He spread bronze-colored hands across the surface. I thanked the Lord for the safety of the barrier between us.

"Why bother interviewing, Phe? I'm your man. I'm as good as it gets and I wouldn't charge you what the others will." His voice was a whispered caress.

"Maybe I've already hired someone," I lied.

"Who? Lyle Greenspan's already committed. He's working on a project for the Museum of Modern Art and Felicia Michaels is in Egypt. You wouldn't use Earl Kincaid. He's not exactly dependable."

"And I wouldn't use you, either, for the same

reason," I said firmly. I picked up the receiver and punched in a number. "Whit, please show Mr. Hernandez out."

Damon leaned in, placing his copper-colored face very close to mine. I could smell the heat emanating from him and the aroma of coffee on his breath. He probably still took it black.

"I am not ready to leave, Phe," he said, without any inflection in his tone. "You need me. Let bygones be bygones and hire me. We always made a good team."

Although there was no longer a "we," the idea of working with Damon again was tempting, but not to be considered. Only masochists would hitch their wagons to his.

Whit, still standing at the door, cleared her throat. "Phoenix, do you need me?"

"Yes, Mr. Hernandez is ready to leave. Please help him find his way out."

"I'm not done," Damon said again, his voice even. I wondered about this new calmness.

He took a couple of long strides toward my assistant, who seemed spellbound by his physique. Her eyes practically bugged out of her head.

Damon placed a hand on Whit's arm and eased her out of the doorway, firmly shutting the door in her face. Not in the mood to be alone with him, I picked up the phone.

"I'll call the police and have you removed," I threatened.

He reached a hand out for the receiver. "One minute, Phe. Listen to what I have to say."

I'd never been one to take orders. That came from living with four bossy brothers who would run over me if I let them. I'd learned one thing at an early age: if you wanted to be heard, and respected, either you spoke up or fought back. So hoping to send him a message I was not to be toyed with, I grabbed Damon's arm, right below the crease of the elbow and applied pressure.

His sharp intake of breath told me I'd accomplished my mission. I relinquished my hold and his entire body relaxed.

The moment I let go, Damon's free hand clamped down on mine. "Hang up, Phe," he ordered.

My reflexes kicked in and my hand opened of its own accord. The receiver catapulted, clunking against Damon's temple.

Startled, I reached out to press my fingers against the injured flesh. I hadn't meant to hit him that hard.

"Oh, Damon, I'm sorry."

We exchanged a long, charged look. Damon's fingers remained twined around my wrist. Sympathy was not what he was after.

"That hot temper hasn't mellowed with age, I see," he said more amiably than I would have.

"It was an accident, I'm sorry. But if you hadn't manhandled me it would never have happened."

"Manhandled you? I reached across to touch you, *chica.*" Smoky gray eyes swept my face. Blood thudded in my ears. *Damon Hernandez could no longer get to me.* I repeated it like a mantra.

And *chica* wasn't going to work. Not this time. Using my free hand, I poured water from my water bottle on some tissues and tossed them to him.

Damon held the wad against his bruised temple. "Sorry doesn't cut it."

"That's all you're getting."

It *was* all he was getting. And, yes, I *was* sorry I'd hurt him. But he'd hurt me badly, too. It had taken me forever to recover from Damon's betrayal.

But I'd filed that painful experience under "Lessons Learned," and cautioned myself never to give my heart to a man who thought that women weren't equal.

And I had learned some things from the experience: independence and resilience. How many African-American twenty-eight-year-old females could say they owned their own business? How many twenty-eight-year-olds owned anything at all?

Damon took another step toward me.

I stepped back.

He advanced.

"I'm not going to get on my knees and plead for forgiveness, if that's what you're thinking," I jabbered, feeling like a cornered rat. This was my office. My studio. I was still in control.

"Then make it up to me in another way," Damon said, his voice deceptively low. "Take me to Tibet with you."

"When hell freezes over."

"Oh, Phe," Damon said, shaking his head and pressing his advantage. One hand still held the wad of tissues against his temple. "Admit you need me."

A morsel of guilt finally kicked in and with it my normal compassion. "Maybe you should have that…uh…injury looked at by a doctor. I'll pick up the tab, of course."

"It'll heal."

He balled up the tissues and tossed it at me. I deftly caught it. For a brief moment I considered stuffing it down his arrogant throat. But I'd done enough damage for one day.

He reached around me and picked up the newspaper, reading out loud.

"'Maitreya, "Future Buddha," one of a price-less trio, found on the grounds of a deserted Tibetan monastery.' Now that's intriguing stuff."

He took his time reading the article while I seethed. After he was through, he uncapped a pen and scribbled some words down on a card before thrusting it at me.

"By the way, Maitreya's supposed to be yellow. That statue has a greenish tinge to it. Here's my home and cell numbers. You'll need my help."

We were on the same wavelength, always had been. The idol did look more green than yellow, but I'd be damned if I'd agree with him out loud.

Tucking my newspaper under his arm, Damon flashed me a grin and wiggled his fingers.

"I'll be waiting to hear from you, Phe. Don't keep me hanging, I'm a pretty busy boy."

He backed out of the room, taking the paper with him. My paper.

Damon would be waiting a damn long time for my call. I certainly didn't want him involved in any project I was associated with.

Yet seeing him after all these years made me realize a few things. It made me grateful and proud that I'd had the courage to end the relationship. If I hadn't walked I wouldn't be where I was today.

Time to get focused and make some phone calls. I needed an X-ray infrared specialist and I needed one soon. I got out my BlackBerry, scrolled through the list of names and found Lyle Greenspan's, Felicia Michaels's and Earl Kincaid's. I quickly scribbled down their numbers.

Fifteen minutes later I conceded Damon was right. All three were busy and unable to make it.

What choice was I left with?

Taking a deep breath, I picked up the phone again. As I punched in the numbers, I thought about my throwing arm. Damon's temple was probably really swollen now, and most likely hurt like hell. *Good; let him suffer for once.*

Damon's voice mail kicked in and I left a message.

Less than five minutes later he called me back.

"What's up, Phe?"

"Where are you, Damon?"

"Heading home?"

"Do you have a visa?" I almost choked on my words. I pictured him grinning.

"Why do I need a visa?"

"Stop playing games."

He'd known all along that I would get back to him. Not only was he eminently qualified, I'd found out during my conversation with Lyle that Damon had converted to Buddhism, Tibet's most popular religion. That, to my mind, was an added advantage. He would at least be familiar with the culture and he wasn't expecting an exorbitant salary.

"You there, Phe? Did you say you want me to go to Tibet with you?"

"Yes. I need your services."

"Cool. Sounds like the perfect assignment for someone like me, a follower of the Dalai Lama."

"Last I knew you were Roman Catholic. Your mother must have had a cow when you converted to Buddhism."

"My mother died. It hasn't been the best of times lately. Buddhism was my salvation, especially after you left me." He chuckled.

Left him? More like the other way around. Damon had made it difficult for me to stay with him, especially if I wanted to remain my own woman. He'd let his machismo get in the way—of everything. But I was sorry to hear of his mother's death. She and I had gotten along well. She had enjoyed regaling me with stories of growing up in the Dominican Republic. And I'd enjoyed every last one of them.

"I'm so sorry about your mom, Damon." I quickly changed the topic. "You and I may very well be on the same wavelength when it comes to Maitreya. I'm thinking this discovery may be a hoax."

"So we go and find out. Why turn down a trip to a country I've been dying to see? You did say all expenses are paid?"

I had not. But I guess he knew that pretty much came with the territory.

Damon continued. "Do you know what finding Maitreya means to the Buddhist world? It means the awaited teacher is coming. He is the master of wisdom, and a guide for people of every religion. Maitreya is supposed to be reborn during a period of decline. He represents our future." He sounded really excited.

I wasn't particularly religious, but the idol's discovery couldn't have been timelier. Natural disasters happened almost daily now and terrorism, well, that was something we lived with. The world needed a savior.

While doing my research, I'd read some of the more "out there" papers. There had been signs of Maitreya's imminent arrival for some time now.

Damon's interest in this project most likely had to do with him wanting to identify the statue as a hoax. And if by some amazing turn of events it was not, then he wanted to be the one to return it to the Dalai Lama.

"We're leaving in two days," I said. "Can you be ready?"

"That's sudden. Has something happened?"

"No. I just wanted to get a jump on things. The sooner the better."

"I can't commit this soon," he said. "I'm in the middle of another project." He was going to keep me dangling. Make me sweat a little.

I expressed myself loudly using a colorful expletive then decided it was pointless letting him needle me. "Make yourself available," I said. "It'll be worth your while."

"Tsk. Such unladylike behavior. How can anyone work with you?"

I repeated the invective. "Do you want the job or not?"

He wanted it. He'd already admitted it was a dream come true.

"Only if the money is right."

I let the silence drag on then countered with a salary that was way too low.

"No way. Up it another thirty percent and there's room for discussion. I gotta go."

"Don't you hang up on me!"

Several beats went by.

"You still there?" he asked.

"I'm here," I said grumpily. "I'll split my bonus. But that means the project has to come in on time or I'll be all over you."

"Now you're talking."

"Go get a visa."

"I'll see what I can do." He disconnected.

I closed my eyes and tried to calm down.

He was still irksome as ever. Why after all this time was Damon Hernandez back in my life?

Someone up there must have it in for me.

Chapter 2

"Bye, Dad. I love you."

"Be safe, little girl."

My dad's voice, the booming, authoritative voice, reduced to a whisper, now sounding lifeless; a mere echo of what it once had been. But at least he was talking. I blew him a kiss through the phone's mouthpiece and disconnected.

If I accomplished only one thing in Tibet, it would be clearing his name. My dad would not have been involved in any type of plot to steal an artifact, especially a Buddha statue lent to a museum in the United States and on his watch. It was ludicrous.

I had a feeling this was going to be the trip of two lifetimes—mine and my dad's.

Tossing my cell phone into my backpack, I navigated the crowded airline terminal and went in search of Damon. I hadn't seen him at the gate's boarding area. The final boarding announcements were now being made. Damon was still nowhere in sight. *Please, God, don't let him let me down.*

There were a few passengers hovering around the counter when I reluctantly boarded the aircraft, none of them Damon. I flopped into the vacant seat next to Althea. The minute the seat belt sign went off, and the flight attendant announced it was safe to get up, I flew out of my uncomfortable coach seat and went in search of Damon. I got to the seat Whit had reserved for Damon, one over the wing with more legroom, and sufficiently far from me. I found a woman seated there.

Damn him! Now what was I going to do?

"Try first class. Those passengers are usually the first ones on," Althea suggested when I returned. "You and I arrived late."

I shot her a puzzled look. "What would he be doing there?"

The Tibetan government hadn't sprung for expensive seats. We were a team, we sat together.

"Who knows?" Her expression indicated she was holding back.

Sauntering by a bewildered flight attendant, I whisked through the curtain separating coach from first and sashayed into the cabin.

"Miss," the attendant called after me. "Miss, there's a bathroom in the back."

"I'm looking for a friend," I tossed over my shoulder.

I stood at the back getting my bearings. No, impossible, that could not be Damon's silver-streaked curls in 3B. That would not be him seated with his feet up on the recliner. On his tray table were a bottle of brand-name water and a plate of appetizers. Back in coach we still hadn't seen anything looking remotely like food.

"Hey," I said, presenting myself. "When did you get here?" I swiped a canapé off his plate and bit into it. "Not bad!"

"Phe," Damon greeted me as if we were the best of friends. "How nice of you to visit." He raised his water bottle in a jaunty salute. "Sorry I missed the briefing. Bad traffic on the expressway. I made the flight by the skin of my teeth. My seat was released. I had to plead, cajole but finally persuaded someone to upgrade me."

Nothing had changed. He'd always had a problem with tardiness. I bit into the canapé wishing it was Damon's head. He removed his feet from the recliner and gestured to the plate.

"Help yourself to as many as you would like."

My stomach was growling, but I wouldn't give Damon the satisfaction of cleaning up all of his leftovers. I'd humbled myself enough, practically begging him to take this job and then splitting my bonus with him. What was wrong with me? I needed my head examined.

"Come on back," I invited, although it damn near choked me. "Althea and I can fill you in on the briefing."

He made a production of yawning. I wanted to slap him. "Can't it wait until after I nap?" He propped one leg over the other so that I could see his fancy slipper socks with the airline's logo. "A nap will do us both some good. You're starting to look a bit peaked, Phe."

I shot him a look that could freeze water and sashayed off. I was up anyway, and needed to work off my frustration.

In the main cabin, the fancy word for coach, there wasn't any sign of food or beverages being served. I wasn't just ravenous now but thirsty, as well. Stopping by my row, I mouthed to Althea, "I'm taking a walk."

"Might as well," she answered in a too-loud voice, which meant music vibrated through the headphones she'd clamped on. "It's going to be a bitch of a flight."

"Flights," I corrected. "We have a connection to face."

Althea groaned, "Oh, God, I hate flying."

My sentiments exactly but I wasn't going to let something like that get in the way. The discomfort would be worth it if what I suspected was true. Maybe, just maybe, the father I loved more than life itself would finally be able to exorcise his demons and join the real world again.

My father, my inspiration, had undergone a tremendous personality change since he'd been fired from his museum curator's job. He'd pushed me to be the best I could be, and instilled in me a sense of independence. It was at his insistence I pursued a career in art restoration, a field that required endless hours of intense concentration and tedious attention to detail. That repetition helped me with discipline.

Dad's losing his job at the museum had been a major blow to his ego and psyche. It had changed the strong yet gentle man I knew into someone unrecognizable. Seeing what losing his job had done to him was so painful. Now those chronic bouts of depression had left him at times incapable of getting out of bed or taking care of basic everyday needs. His job, his art, his museum, his reputation had been everything to him.

I wanted my confident, loving dad back again. When Bhaisajyaguru had been reported missing, Dad had been vilified by the newspapers and branded as either incompetent or in cahoots with the thieves. My mission now was to make him whole again.

I just hoped I wasn't too late.

We had five long hours to go before touching down in Frankfurt, then another long flight to Kathmandu and finally to Lhasa.

At the back galley, I paused. Flight attendants were pulling out beverage carts, and long lines were beginning to form at the lavatories. An attractive African-American attendant handed me a disposable cup filled with liquid.

"You look thirsty," she said.

I thanked her, gulped the drink, and out of my peripheral vision noticed a passenger wending his way toward me. He loped down the aisle with purpose then stopped abruptly at the magazine rack, scanning the offerings. I finished my drink and set down my cup on the galley counter, considering what lay ahead.

The Buddha statue must already be uncrated, photographed and recorded by a registrar. It would need to be analyzed so that an exact date could be put to the piece. Materials would need to be tested to determine the best and safest way to treat, clean and restore the idol. But the actual hard work would begin once I'd decided how best to repair it. It would probably require endless retouching.

An elbow jostled me. Liquid spilled. No apology followed.

"Dang! Excuse you."

I stepped aside. The same passenger who'd been scrutinizing the magazine rack whipped through the galley and made a U-turn up the far aisle.

Rudeness made my blood boil! Instinctively my hands went to the pocket of my cargo pants where I kept my wallet. No fancy purses for me. The wallet was gone, along with my money, credit cards and driver's license. My passport and other important documents were in the knapsack under my seat.

Okay, he'd headed up the other aisle. I strode there with purpose, nudging several grumbling passengers aside.

"Sorry," I mumbled.

"Hey, what's the problem? It's not like you're going anywhere faster than the rest of us," a bespectacled man cried as I bumped into him.

"Miss," a flight attendant called. "Is there

something I can help you with? Are you looking for someone?"

Several passengers craned their necks. One of the flight attendants began trailing me. She probably thought I was deranged or a new breed of terrorist.

I spotted the man who'd stolen my stuff as he hurdled into the middle seat, closed his eyes and pretended to sleep. I leaned over the heavyset man occupying the aisle seat and held out my hand.

"You have something that's mine. Give it up."

The thief opened his eyes and grunted something in a foreign language.

"What's going on?" the other occupant, a woman who was clearly terrified, asked, clutching her chest.

I had no time for explanations. My wallet had been there when I boarded the plane. I'd produced my driver's license at the gate. My passport and plane ticket had been put back into my backpack after I'd checked in. I needed my money and I needed my ID, simple as that.

"Give me back my wallet," I said, reaching across the obese man and grabbing a handful of the thief's shirt. His eyes bugged out of his head and his neck jerked forward as I began to shake him.

"Turn it over, now."

I'd garnered pretty much all of the attention of the passengers in the surrounding areas.

The pickpocket's mouth worked. He made a gargling sound. The woman seated next to him's left eye ticked. Petrified, she pressed her bony body against the wall.

I straddled the male passenger and stood in front of the thief, hemming him in. Behind me, bedlam broke out. I felt a hand tapping my shoulder.

"Miss, you need to calm down."

Audible gasps followed as the surrounding people watched me shove a finger into the hollow of my accoster's throat. His entire body jerked as he gasped for air and made a gurgling sound.

"I'll stick my knee in your groin next," I said, patting him down with my free hand. "Hand over my wallet."

I felt a bulky object at his waistband. Victorious, I reached into his pants and retrieved my goods then waved my wallet above his head.

"As I suspected, you took something that's not yours."

"Take it easy, little lady," a Southern voice growled from behind me. "You keep this up and we'll need to restrain you."

I glanced over my shoulder, spotting one of

the pilots. I eased the pressure on the pickpocket's windpipe.

"This man's a thief. He stole my wallet," I explained.

The thief held his throat, rasping. Guttural
words came out in the strange foreign language.

"Is that so," the pilot said, sounding as if he
didn't quite believe me.

I held up my wallet, doing a quick check to
make sure that my money, credit cards, driver's
license and social security card were still in their
respective compartments.

The pilot attempted to interrogate the man but
the passenger didn't respond. Orders were given
to find a crew member proficient in Chinese.

"I want to press charges," I said, as yet another
flight attendant came racing up the aisle to the
pilot's assistance.

"We'll call ahead and have the authorities meet
the flight. These things take time, so you'll
probably miss your connection if you have one,"
she answered.

I couldn't afford to be delayed. Timing on this
project was everything. I'd promised to have
Maitreya, if that's who the statue was, restored
before Buddha's Enlightenment Day. That
festival drew every pilgrim from the far ends of
the earth. It also helped fuel the Tibetan economy.

So although it went against everything I believed in to let the crook go free, what choice did I have? I didn't have time for questions or filling out tedious paperwork. I could not afford to miss my connection. I had a deadline to meet. Missing my connection would cost me money.

And possibly my father's sanity and his name.

But why had the pickpocket chosen me of all people to come after? I was dressed in cargo pants and hiking boots, not exactly an outfit that was a fashion statement or said I had money to burn.

Grumbling, I flounced by the still-gawking passengers. Their loud whispers followed me back to my row. A few even had the gumption to cheer.

"Way to go!"

"You're some gutsy female."

I grunted something and sank into my seat and quickly clamped on my headphones. Music would soothe the soul and make me forget how ravenous I was.

My pickpocket disappeared in Frankfurt and we finally made it to Lhasa, Tibet, without further incident.

After enduring immigration we collected our checked luggage and cleared customs. When we finally exited the Gonkar terminal, I looked around for our driver. Several Asian men held placards with names that were barely legible. There was no sign of a driver retained for just the Sutherland group.

"Xiong Jing, our project manager, said he'd arranged transportation for our group," I said out loud. "But there doesn't seem to be anyone here to meet us."

I was tired, edgy and wound up from the ridiculous incident. I hadn't gotten much sleep on the flight, not folded like a pretzel in those uncomfortable seats.

"I don't see anyone waiting," Damon said, coming up behind me.

"Could be he's late. I'll see what we can do about getting us to the hotel."

"I'll get a taxi." Damon hurried off.

"I'm finding rickshaws," I announced. "They're cheaper and a whole lot more fun." I stomped off in the other direction, my trusty Althea, her dreads secured by a rubber band, next to me.

"I hope the luggage and equipment fit into those rickety pedicabs," Damon said as he returned loud enough for me to hear. "Betcha anything Phoenix will make that luggage fit."

I decided to let it go.

A weathered-looking man of indeterminate age stepped in front of me. "Madam Sutherland?" he queried in a singsongy voice with foreign intonations.

"I am. And you are?"

"Your driver. Your manager, Xiong Jing, asked me to meet you. I'm sorry I was detained. Is that all of your luggage?"

My manager? I waved a hand indicating the group and their bags. "Yes, thank you for coming to get us."

Everyone had been instructed to travel light. We were restricted to clothing and personal effects, enough to fit in either backpacks or duffels. The bulky items we'd been forced to check were the equipment we would need to work.

The driver signaled to a group of lounging porters. The men swooped down like vultures, piling the bags and equipment on their heads and backs. They gestured for us to follow them.

Outside, a minibus was haphazardly parked at the curb, hemming in a line of beat-up taxis. A child who looked to be no older than twelve guarded the vehicle. Coins exchanged hands before our escort motioned to us to climb in.

I was short of breath and my chest felt tight. I blamed the long, exhausting flights and the twelve-thousand-foot altitude for this unexpected weariness. After the bags and equipment were crammed into the back hatch we pulled out.

A nerve-racking journey followed. The bus swerved this way and that, narrowly missing pedestrians, bicyclists and pedicabs. We bounced down rutted streets and with every jostle the cardboard airline meal I'd ingested threatened to be expelled. I pretended to take it all in stride but what I really needed was a Tums, something to settle my chest and stomach that were in danger of imploding.

Ten minutes passed then the driver pulled over abruptly.

"Where are we?"

"Please just make it the hotel," Althea mumbled, opening up two droopy eyes. She looked about as gray as I probably did.

I couldn't quite make out where we were. It was dark outside. Where we'd stopped sure didn't look like the Himalaya Hotel to me. Squinting, I spotted a barricade. It must be some kind of a security checkpoint of sorts.

A uniformed man, police or public security, I think they were called, approached. He waved his arms and demanded something of the driver in Tibetan.

The driver sprang from the vehicle. His stance quickly became subservient as he spoke to the man before motioning for us to get out.

"Hey, what's going on?" I asked.

When the driver didn't answer, I climbed from the bus and followed him.

A number of uniformed men converged on my driver, jabbering and pointing to the back of the van where the luggage was piled. They began motioning to unload the bags and equipment. The men went through our personal items, tossing clothing on the ground and waving electronic gadgets in the air.

"I'm falling asleep on my feet," Althea complained. "Let them take what they want."

"Are those real guns?" I asked, shock receding.

I'd read about the Public Security Bureau, Tibet's answer to the police, and figured these rather unpleasant men were them. I'd been told they wore green uniforms but favored plainclothes and dark glasses when undercover. Their goal was to blend in with the crowd, and so they would often hide behind newspapers. The PSB's responsibilities encompassed staying on the alert for civil unrest, checking for expired visas and monitoring crime and traffic.

A bald, beefy officer, who looked to be the leader, unzipped Damon's duffel and began strewing clothes about. I chuckled gleefully as two pairs of jeans and a handful of T-shirts went flying. When sweatshirts hit the dirty pavement, followed by socks and a pitiful few pairs of underwear, I heard Damon groan. Beefy, the larger man, waved something that got the attention of the other officers.

Things got pretty serious quickly and my good humor ended. Heart in my mouth, I watched security converge.

"Dammit, Damon," I gritted out through clenched teeth. "Tell me you weren't stupid enough to smuggle in booze or drugs?"

"Just a dime bag of pot for medicinal purposes," he quipped. An amused grin lit up his pretty boy features. The man didn't seem to sweat. I, however, was sweating plenty.

The driver continued jabbering away in his language to the Tibetan officers. He beckoned Damon over.

The officers held up two books. I squinted, hoping to get a look at the jackets. I came closer while the officers kept their flashlights trained on us. Both books were written by popular *New York Times* bestseller authors.

But it wasn't the books the officers were after. It was the photographs used as bookmarks they shook out from between the pages. Damon must have forgotten them there. He'd used photos of the exiled Dalai Lama to mark pages. He'd probably forgotten them there. This was what the fuss was about.

"What's the problem?" I asked the driver.

A crooked index finger worried the driver's forehead. "It's illegal to have pictures of the Dalai Lama," he explained. "You all may be in big trouble and so am I."

Damon thudded his palms against his head. "I'll take full responsibility if you explain to the officers it was an oversight on my part," he said. "Tell them we're here on official government business."

The driver sighed loudly. "I'm not sure that's going to work. This isn't the United States."

Turning back to the officers, his palms clamped together as if he were praying, he apparently pleaded our cause. The more he spoke, the more questions were hurled at him.

I needed to do something. I couldn't just stand there. I trotted over just as the lead officer snarled something at the driver.

"They won't deal with a woman," my driver yelped in loud English, gesticulating with one hand for me to stay out of it.

I handed him an envelope. "Explain to these gentlemen we're not ordinary tourists. We've been commissioned by the government to work on an important historical finding."

The envelope was snatched out of his hand by Beefy, and a flashlight produced. The surrounding officers peered at the paper and began talking at once.

"They don't read English," my driver explained. "They don't understand."

"Then please translate," I pleaded. "Show them the official government stamp." I pointed to the letter's gold seal.

"I will do my best," he said firmly, as if fearing I would make things worse. "Tibet is not exactly a woman's world."

"It doesn't seem to be a man's, either," I muttered then turned away and fumbled through the pockets of my pants.

Behind me Damon muttered. I called on the Lord for patience. What I really wanted to do was throttle Damon.

My barb was apparently lost on the driver, who was out of his element. In a desperate attempt to move things along, I whipped out a copy of the newspaper article I'd been saving. I pointed to the picture of the future Buddha, patted my chest, and pointed to the letter again.

This served to elicit more excited conversation.

"Talk to me," Damon said to our driver. "What's happening?"

"They're thinking of arresting both of you," our driver explained. "You, for illegal possession of the Dalai Lama photographs, and her for obstructing justice."

"This can't be happening, Phe," Damon snapped.

No point in getting into it with him, or telling him it was his fault. I needed to come up with a plan. I looked over at Althea and she looked scared stiff and silent.

I raced over to the area where the luggage was strewn. Two of the security police followed, guns trained on me. I riffled through my knapsack and dumped the remaining contents on the ground. Finding what I needed, I turned back to them.

These were men. I was a woman. In their minds I served no useful purpose, except one.

My voice became sweet and seductive as I spoke to our driver. "Tell them I have a very special present, something I brought all the way from America."

I began passing around the cigars I held. The remaining one I stuck in my mouth.

"Got a light?" I asked Beefy, stroking his arm and making a motion with my fingers, indicating I needed a match.

Beefy smiled and produced matches. He stuck his cigar into his mouth while his eyes roamed over me. Then he lit his before mine. The other officers followed his lead and began lighting up.

Sucking on that smelly thing, I batted my eye-lashes at Beefy, then tilted my head back and exhaled a perfect smoke ring. The officers tried to imitate me, but didn't quite make it. I exhaled again, pouting my lips.

Nice lips, I'd often been told.

"Now," I said to the driver. "Can you tell Handsome I think he's hot? And if it's okay with him I'd like to go. He can visit with me if he'd like."

There was a gleam of admiration in the driver's eye as he nodded and began speaking with Beefy, who kept his eyes on me the whole time. Finally he jerked a thumb in the direction of the minivan.

I signaled to the crew and raced toward the vehicle. There would be fat chance of that man ever seeing me again. Not if I could help it.

Damon cleared his throat as we climbed back into the bus. I ignored him. He should be thanking me for saving his miserable butt. He should be drawing my bath and kissing my toes.

But knowing my ex, he would never acknowledge that I'd saved the day. Pride and machismo had always been his undoing.

"Thank you, Phe," he said, surprising me. "That was quick thinking on your part."

I almost swallowed my tongue but managed a nod in his direction. Him, thanking me, was unheard of. *Maybe, he'd changed.*

Nah, best not to go there. Damon had his own agenda.

And I had mine.

Chapter 3

"What do you mean there's been a holdup on the project? Why didn't anyone call me?" I asked Xiong Jing, our project manager, when I met with him in the lobby the next morning.

"These things happen, madam. You are to enjoy your stay at the hotel until you hear otherwise."

I was ready to go to work. A delay would mean my bonus was in jeopardy, the one I'd foolishly agreed to split. Turning my brown-eyed gaze on Xiong Jing, I said, "I'm Phoenix, not madam. I'd appreciate it if you'd remember that."

He bowed his head in acknowledgment. "As you wish."

Xiong Jing, our project manager, was an Oxford-educated man in his late thirties. I'd disliked him on sight and I got the feeling the sentiment was mutual. There was something about the way he refused to look me in the eye.

His behavior hadn't fazed Damon one bit. He'd shrugged, dismissing the man's aloof body language as a cultural thing. But I thought there was more to it than that. I was certain Xiong Jing disliked females and black females at that.

So why hadn't he told me there was a problem last evening when he'd called and arranged this meeting?

I studied the elaborate chandelier in the hotel lobby and prayed for patience—not one of my better virtues. That little problem had cost me an assignment or two.

I'd convinced my travel companions to sleep in, reminding them that this might be their one night in the lap of luxury. Future accommodations would be at the monastery in refurbished monks' and nuns' cells. Luxuries such as comfortable beds didn't come with that territory.

"I can arrange tours of our beautiful city for you and your group, madam," Xiong Jing offered, his eyes not quite meeting mine.

"Why don't you just tell me what's happening?" I asked, trying my best to tamp down on my irritation. What I really wanted to do was reach over, grab the man's chin, and force him to look at me.

"Security's been increased around the monastery," Xiong Jing answered through an almost-closed mouth. "Rumor has it there was a bomb threat."

"I guess it would make some serious statement, blowing up the Deprung Monastery where the Maitreya is being housed."

He didn't seem that perturbed at the thought. "We live in an era of terrorism," Xiong Jing said. "The discovery of Maitreya—considered 'the future'—is bound to cause unrest. If you have political or social changes there are always disbelievers. Humans will sacrifice themselves for the cause."

Was there a hidden meaning behind this? I didn't have time to interpret double entendres, if that's what it was. I'd reflect on Xiong Jing's words later.

"So what do we do?" I asked. "Sit at this hotel and twiddle our thumbs until you contact us?"

"Madam, you can, or you can go on one of our tours and learn something about my country. That might be the smart thing to do until things calm down."

I didn't like his tone or the implication that I

knew very little about his country. I also didn't like it that he was perfectly accepting of the delay.

"Surely there's someone else I can talk to," I fumed. "Where is Liu Bangfu, the Minister of Religion and Culture? Will he not be meeting with us?"

"The minister is busy dealing with the police and such," Xiong Jing responded smoothly. "I promised him I would take very good care of you. And I will."

I took a step toward the smarmy project manager. A muscle in his jaw flickered. He stepped back, keeping an acceptable space between us. He probably wasn't used to anyone getting in his face, especially a woman.

"Why don't you take me to the police?" I asked, softening my tone a bit. "I'd like to hear what they're doing about this bomb threat."

"Madam, I can't."

"Why not?"

"Phe, are you badgering our project manager?" Damon's amused voice came from behind me.

I turned to find him only feet away, so close I could smell the combination of body heat and musk, his characteristic scent. He'd been jogging. His silver-streaked curls were plastered to his head and sweat trickled down his solar plexus. In some ways, I'd once thought he was the best-looking man I knew. I still did.

Raising a corded arm, Damon took a swig from a foam cup he was carrying.

I shot him a disgusted look and turned my attention back to Xiong Jing.

"Don't let her bully you," Damon said, trying to be the peacemaker and buddying up to the man.

"Stay out of this."

Xiong Jing, happy to have an ally, chuckled. "Ms. Phoenix is in no way bullying me. She has been most gracious." He was comfortable with his own gender. He repeated to Damon what he'd just told me.

Damon pumped both arms in the air. "A small reprieve, a chance to go sightseeing. Buddha is good. And so is this magnificent hotel." Grabbing my elbow, he attempted to propel me along. "*Chica,* you and I are going out on the town. I'll even spring for breakfast."

"I've had breakfast," I snarled. "I need to find the Minister of Religion and Culture."

"Find him later." Damon made a production of sniffing under his armpits. "Turning me down, Phe? I guess I do need a shower."

Despite my earlier irritation with him I laughed. He really was pitiful. Pitiful but funny. It was one of the things I had liked about him. He pretty much took everything in stride.

Besides, having Damon with us might come in

useful after all. I was slowly finding out that being a female in this male-dominated city, dubbed the Roof of the World, was not going to be a picnic.

Two hours later after breakfast and leaving Damon to sightsee solo, I was seated in a crumbling old Tibetan building on the east side of Lhasa. Xiong Jing, who reluctantly agreed to accompany me here, paced the austere waiting room of the minister's office. The expression on his face was inscrutable. Three puny miniature golden yaks, encased in glass, were considered decoration.

Tossing aside the newspaper I'd been pretending to read, I approached a petite secretary who was hunting and pecking on an old typewriter.

She was Chinese, and took her duties seriously, guarding the Minister of Religion and Culture like a zealous Foo Dog. So far she'd managed to keep me at bay by insisting Liu Bangfu was still meeting with the chief of police. The typewriter she banged on I hadn't seen the likes of in years. No fancy technology here.

The secretary looked up nervously when I approached.

I drummed my fingers on her ancient desk and stared her down.

"Yes, madam?"

"I'm giving the minister another five minutes then I'm going in," I said.

Scooting her chair back a safe distance, she squeaked, "Mr. Bangfu has given me strict orders that he is not to be interrupted."

I straightened my five-foot-nine-inch frame. "Please remind him that I've been waiting here almost an hour," I said, leaning in closer. She seemed to shrink.

Xiong Jing was still pacing. He darted worried looks at me. Judging by his mottled complexion, he would have preferred to be anywhere but here.

"I'm counting to ten, then I'm going in," I said, beginning to count softly.

The frightened secretary picked up the receiver but hesitated before inserting a finger into the rotary dial.

Grabbing the receiver from her, I announced, "Ten," and planted it back into its cradle. Leaving her openmouthed, I stalked by her and wended my way down a long corridor. Heels thudded behind me as Xiong Jing followed.

I stuck my head into the first open door and called, "Hello, sorry to interrupt. I've been waiting outside for quite some time."

A middle-aged Chinese man held a receiver in one hand. He barked something into the mouthpiece before dropping it into its cradle. The brass nameplate on his desk confirmed that he was Liu Bangfu.

"Mr. Bangfu," I said, pointedly glancing at my watch. "I thought perhaps you had forgotten me."

An eyebrow rose. "Ms. Sutherland, welcome. You are the American restorer?"

The emphasis placed on *American* did not go unnoticed.

"Yes, I'm Phoenix Sutherland."

"My apologies. Didn't your project manager tell you a situation came about I needed to handle?" His natural graciousness kicking in, he stuck out his hand. "A pleasure to meet you, madam."

I accepted that hand, squeezing it hard enough to make him realize I wasn't just some girlie-girl.

"May I offer you soja, our tea?" the minister asked, actually wincing. Gently he pried his hand loose and picked up the receiver again.

"Bring us tea," he ordered into the phone, no doubt addressing the secretary.

"I'd just like to be told what's going on and what the reason is for this delay," I insisted.

The minister and Xiong Jing exchanged looks. For a moment I thought neither would answer.

"This bomb threat has us all nervous and aware," Liu Bangfu said carefully.

"Isn't the chief of police involved? What is he doing about this? I thought you were meeting with him."

That produced another set of glances.

"Ten Seng Yang and I conducted our business over the phone. Have a seat."

I sat in the one chair facing Bangfu and waited for him to go on. When no further explanation followed, I added, "Please tell me what's going on?"

Liu Bangfu's glasses slid dangerously low on his nose. He fidgeted with them then finally gave up. I could tell he wasn't used to explaining himself to a woman and didn't like it one bit.

"Didn't I say the police are looking into it?" he said, the corners of his mouth turned up in what was supposed to be a smile. "I am certain they will keep us informed."

"And just what are they looking into?"

"They're interrogating groups that are known to be disruptive."

A shriek came from the doorway. The noise sounded like a panic-stricken cat. We all jumped. The annoying secretary came scurrying in, arms flapping.

"Sir, sir," she squeaked, hopping from one high-heeled foot to another. "We need to leave the building. Now. There's been a bomb threat."

"What!" Bangfu was up like a shot, gathering the papers on his desk. "You'd better leave," he said, bolting from behind its safety. My project manager, who'd forgotten he had promised to take good care of me, raced after him.

Bangfu's secretary's high-pitched voice carried. "I got an anonymous call from a man who said a bomb was planted in the building. I telephoned the police. They told me to get out now. Come, come, we must go."

I could be hardheaded but I wasn't a fool. I sprinted right after her, but instead of leaping onto the creaky elevator they were all taking, I raced down three flights of stairs. I almost got run over by a number of uniformed men wearing visors and gloves on their way up.

I burst out of the building and spotted the majority of people milling around on the other side of the street. Neither Bangfu, my project manager, nor the minister's high-strung secretary were among them. Suddenly I spun around.

Was I imagining things?

I couldn't shake the feeling I was being watched. I looked across the street and into the eyes of the pickpocket who'd attempted to steal my wallet on the plane. He took off running.

Without looking right or left I gave chase, darting across the street and right in front of a pedicab. The driver swerved, cursing at me. I was fast losing sight of my accoster. Pushing people aside, I raced after him, and came damn close to catching him, when I tripped and fell. By the time I'd steadied myself, he was plowing through the crowd.

I continued my pursuit. Brakes squealed and cars swerved as I wove through the traffic. Foreign curses came at me from every direction. Bent and determined as I was that he would not get away, I sprinted in front of a bus packed with locals. The vehicle swerved in a valiant attempt to avoid running me over.

Frustrated, I watched the thief hop into an idling cab and the vehicle inch its way onto the road.

I couldn't just sit helplessly and let the pickpocket get away, not when there was a car at my disposal.

I spied an idling SUV and dove onto the driver's lap. Opening the door, I pushed him out.

"I need to borrow your car. I'll make it up to you!" I started the ignition and swerved onto the street.

Horns honked and metal scraped metal. I held on to the steering wheel for dear life. Another vehicle clipped the back bumper and the SUV catapulted upward before settling on the sidewalk. I tried steering around the crowd of scattering people and finally slid to a stop in front of a terrified woman clutching the hands of two children.

The mother and children barely had time to make it out of the way before I lost control and the truck plowed headfirst into a brick building. There were popping sounds and a loud explosion.

Then everything around me crumbled in slow motion.

I knew I was alive because there was an acrid smell in my nostrils. I felt hands under my armpits pulling me from the vehicle. I was laid on my back looking up at a darkening sky alive with pyrotechnics. There was a buzz of conversation around me and the bitter taste of smoke in my mouth. My entire body burned.

Memory came back in vivid Technicolor. I had tossed a man out of his car and wrecked it. *What was I thinking?* I would need to make good on that somehow. *Was that even possible?* A huge adrenaline rush forced me into a seated position. I needed to find the man and make amends. Strong arms pushed me back onto the sidewalk and foreign words filled my ears.

In the distance, sirens wailed followed by more popping and loud explosions. Flames spiraled sky-high as people dived for cover. Now I was alone, left to claw my way through mass hysteria, bitter smoke making me choke. The vehicle I'd been in just minutes ago was engulfed in flames and so were several others. I hoped there were no humans inside.

Sick to my stomach, I fought the stream of traffic and retraced my steps, looking for the government building that I'd fled earlier.

My chest felt constricted and my lungs hurt. I passed injured people, and tripped over those way beyond help. I hit a wall of crying, screaming human bodies that police struggled to hold back. Those that still breathed life were being shoveled into the backs of ambulances. Only a charred column of the government building remained. I'd been lucky to get out.

I looked up at the spiraling smoke in disbelief and tuned out the popping and hissing. The skeletonlike building reminded me of a spent sparkler at the culmination of the Fourth of July. But this was not Independence Day and I was far away from the good old U.S. of A. The building I had just been in and had been driving near—had been bombed. Looked like those threats *were* true.

I was surrounded by shocked faces coated in gray-and-white film. For the first time in a long while I did not feel in control of my life. I stood there praying that the obnoxious project manager, the Minister of Religion and Culture and even the vapid secretary had been spared.

Life, sweet life. I breathed in and out, long and deep.

A voice I recognized filtered through the madness. "Madam," Xiong Jing said, tapping me on the arm. "There you are. Are you okay?! I have a hired car. I'll take you back to your hotel."

I hadn't thought it was possible to be this happy to see anyone in my life. I could have easily hugged him.

Turning away from the sight that was destined to haunt me for the rest of my life, I followed Xiong Jing to a side street where several parked cars waited.

I wanted to kiss the sidewalk and give praise to Damon's Buddha.

Chapter 4

"We've been invited to tea at Madeline Wong's," I said, the moment Althea picked up the phone. We'd spent the last day or so confined at the hotel and I was bored. We were still at the Himalaya Hotel and I was going out of my mind. The bombing of the government building and the destruction of the properties around had thrown everyone into a tizzy. I considered myself lucky, having escaped with some minor cuts and bruises. "Think you're up for it?"

Althea's laughter pealed through the earpiece. "Girl, if it means getting out of this room, the answer is a resounding yes."

"Good. Madeline's invited all of us to her home."

"That was nice of her. Is this some fancy dress-up occasion?"

"Just look decent. She's the fabulous woman who's my benefactor and who helped me land this assignment. A car's being sent for us. Can you be ready in an hour?"

"Absolutely."

It turned out being inside the SUV—and the air bag—actually saved me from severe bodily harm. The brick building I hit was near the government office building I had just been in. And the bomb went off right when I lost control of the SUV.

Talk about timing.

Damon had been wonderful to me these last few days. But that didn't mean I trusted him or was in danger of succumbing to his charms.

Now I stood under a blessedly warm shower thinking about my meager wardrobe. Did I have something appropriate to wear to tea at Madeline Wong's house?

I had met the wealthy widow on a plane ages ago when I was returning from Italy to New York. Because of overbooking, I had had the good fortune to be upgraded to business class. Madame Wong had had the lousy luck of being bumped from her first-class seat. She wasn't happy and let the entire business-class section know it.

I'd found the immaculately dressed woman swaddled in furs a bit intimidating. But as it turned out we were both reading the same book, a popular *New York Times* bestseller. That made for easy conversation.

I learned that her annual trip to New York was something she and her late husband had looked forward to. And even though he had died a few years ago, Madame Wong was bound and determined to continue the tradition. She needed her Fifth and Madison Avenues fix.

For the next seven and a half hours I'd heard all about the foundation that she and her dear departed husband had established. I'd listened with particular interest when Madeline spoke of the foundation's vast art collection, rare tapestries and the antiquities the Wongs had inherited or purchased at auction.

In turn, Madame Wong had been delighted to discover I was in the art conservation and restoration business. Credentials unchecked, she'd hired me on the spot to repair some chipped vases from the Ming dynasty, as well as a tapestry that was almost threadbare. Having Madeline Wong as a client had certainly helped my career. I was a relatively new art conservator and this was a huge feather in my cap.

Althea and Damon were in the lobby when I got off the elevator. Damon whistled.

I glared at him. "You know I clean up nice."

"Phe. You look lovely. I've always liked it when you wear your hair in one braid."

"I'm sure," I mumbled ungraciously as he continued to stare. "Madame Wong's car is most likely waiting out front."

A classic silver Mercedes with highly polished chrome was parked at the entrance. A uniformed chauffeur sat at the ready.

Before I could reach for the car door he'd already gotten it. He helped me into the opulent interior, while my two companions crawled in behind me.

"Now this is luxurious," Althea said, her fingers stroking the camel leather.

The door shut behind us. We wound our way through streets that were considerably less congested than my last disastrous venture out.

Everywhere I looked there were mountains. I now knew why Lhasa is considered the highest city in the world. Gratefully, I inhaled large breaths of unpolluted air and gazed up into a sky, a mesmerizing shade of deep blue. I could get used to this.

There was some of the most interesting architecture I'd ever seen. Old and new converged but a strong Chinese influence prevailed. And every-where, just everywhere, were the Buddhist monu-ments.

It was one of the reasons pilgrims were drawn to Lhasa. They especially liked congregating at the Barkhor, which was considered the most famous prayer circuit of them all. Hundreds of people came from afar to be closer to their beliefs. I found it fascinating to watch them chanting, turning their prayer wheels and prostrating themselves.

"What kind of ceremony is that?" I asked, spotting a procession on a side street. A line of men carried what looked to be a person swaddled in white silk scarves. The person was bound to two thin tree trunks while borne through the streets.

"That's a corpse on its way to a sky burial," Damon answered soberly, his jovial mood dissipating.

"Sky burial? I'm not sure I understand."

"Tibetans don't bury their dead like Christians do. They cut the flesh and organs from the dead person's body and feed them to vultures. Sky burials are illegal to watch."

"The vultures tear the flesh of someone's beloved apart? That's gross."

"No grosser than burying someone six feet under for worms to eat. At least this way the dead lives on in some form."

I felt queasy. I could tell from Althea's gray face that nausea was only seconds away.

We continued our journey, eventually reaching the outskirts of town, passing the Deprung Monastery with its four tantric colleges.

We began a steep climb into snowcapped mountains. The scenery changed and became more pastoral. From this height, the views literally took my breath away.

Another abrupt turn had us crawling up an even steeper incline. At the top sat a majestic home with mountains creating a magnificent backdrop. It looked like something out of a painting.

"You have arrived," our chauffeur announced, pulling up in front of an intricately carved front door. He hopped out of the driver's seat and came around to the back.

No sooner had I stepped from the car than a petite woman sailed out of the house and approached the vehicle.

"Phoenix, my darling? Where are you?" Madeline Wong called.

Madeline was charming, shrewd and tough as nails. Her razor-sharp mind cut through the bull and got to the bottom line. I'd once watched her negotiate, and she did it graciously and with a smile, always getting her way.

Even when she and I had talked money, she told

me what she was willing to pay to have her vases and tapestries restored. I countered but she hadn't budged an inch and I'd ended up agreeing to everything she suggested. Although I'd lost a couple of bucks in the process, having her name on my client list more than made up for it. Plus, I'd gained a valuable friend.

Madeline clasped me to her and I was enveloped in a cloud of perfume. Beautiful by Estée Lauder, it had to be. I'd know that scent anywhere. My mother used to wear it.

"Phoenix," she gushed. "Just look at you. Lovelier than ever."

"You look wonderful, as well. Who's the designer?" I took a stab at it. "Vera Wang?" Not that I knew anything about expensive clothing, nor did I care to know.

"No, silly, but close enough. My talented tailor in Hong Kong. This has been in the back of my closet. Where are my manners? Introduce me to your friends."

Althea and Damon were just getting out the back of the Benz. Madeline Wong's heavily mascaraed eyes grew round. "Phoenix, you held out on me. You did not tell me he was—how do you say it?—hot." Her words were loud enough for Damon to hear. His cocky smile and slight nod of acknowledgment told me he hadn't missed a word.

Madeline rambled on, oblivious to the tension between us. "The lady, this very elegant lady, must be your girlfriend Althea. I love your hair," she announced, tweaking one of Althea's locks and embracing her. "See, I have become very Western in my greeting."

After introductions were made, Madame led the way into her home.

"Sit! Sit!" she said when we'd entered a living room almost as big as a church sanctuary. She gestured to several elaborately upholstered chairs and couches piled high with silk cushions. "Make yourself at home."

"Wow!" Damon's exclamation echoed my feelings. "This is some place you have."

It was. What Madame Wong called home looked more like a museum. It didn't take degrees in art history or restoration to know that the hanging tapestries were priceless, some of which I'd repaired in her New York home, the Van Goghs and Picassos real.

"Arif," Madame Wong called to an unseen person. "Our guests are here. We will require tea." Like a queen holding an audience with her minions, she settled in one of the overstuffed chairs. "How are you liking my adopted country? It is a bit different from the United States, yes? It really was time to move on from Italy."

Althea, who appeared awed, gazed around cataloging everything.

"We've been pretty much confined to our hotel," she eventually said. "Every time Phoenix ventures out something catastrophic happens."

Madeline's penciled-in eyebrows arched as high as her ornate ceiling. "I heard the bombing of the ministry. What else has there been?"

"Phoenix, you tell her."

I filled Madeline in on the episode on the plane and the run-in with the guards after leaving the airport.

She was all of a sudden serious. Her French-manicured nails tapped her rouged cheeks.

"And you think this is all being done deliberately? That if you fear for your life you will pack your bags and go home?"

"I think that's the goal."

"What would this person's or these people's motives be?"

Damon, who'd been quiet, spoke up. "Could be that person wants the restoration job. He or she may have something to hide. Something they don't want discovered."

"It's a he if this person is native. Tibet is a chauvinistic place." Madame Wong gracefully stood, yards of chiffon floating around her. She always looked as though she was expecting paparazzi.

"Arif," she called again. "Where are you? My guests are thirsty."

The invisible servant did not respond. Appearing totally disgusted, Madame Wong said, "I may have to go and see what's keeping Arif."

Yet Madeline made no effort to do that. She took her seat again, fabric swishing around her. When she crossed her legs, high-heeled jeweled sandals and bright red toenail polish peeked from under palazzo pants.

"I read there is a legend associated with Maitreya and the other Buddhas in the trio. Can you fill us in?"

Madame Wong twisted rings with gemstones the size of miniature golf balls. "There was a poor family who, supposedly having nothing to give Buddha, offered him a glass of water and their meager dinner. In return, the three sons were reborn. One became Bhaisajyaguru and acquired the ability to heal. The second became Maitreya, known for his benevolence and friendship, and became perhaps the greatest of them all. The third, Manjushri, a Bodhisattva, is said to have the power of discriminating wisdom."

"What makes these statues so valuable?" Damon interrupted, cutting to the chase.

I could tell Madeline was enjoying storytelling. Her eyes had a dreamy look. "Just think, an artisan monk worked on creating these statues his entire life. They were gifted to Tenzin Gyatso, the fourteenth Dalai Lama and stolen from him shortly before he was exiled."

Madame Wong was on her feet again. "Let me see to our tea. Here I am going on and on. Arif, where are you?" She headed off to what I assumed to be the kitchen.

Damon and I exchanged an amused look. Meanwhile Althea roamed the room admiring the antique furniture and rare paintings.

A shrill scream came from someplace close by. It had us running in the direction Madeline Wong had disappeared.

We found her in the cavernous kitchen, her arms flapping, her mouth open wide.

At her feet a dark-skinned man lay prostrate with a nasty bloody bruise to his head. Next to him was a bloody goat's hoof with a piece of paper tacked to it.

Chapter 5

"Take Madame Wong with you into the living room," Damon said, bending over Arif. "She looks like she could use a cup of tea. I'll take over from here."

My friend did seem as if she could use some of the tea she'd been prepared to serve, maybe spiked with hard liquor. Madeline appeared to be in an almost-catatonic state, staring down on her servant. Her spiky eyelashes were the only things that moved.

A hobbling Althea took Madeline by the elbow and gently eased her from the room. I remained where I was. No way was I leaving Damon's side.

Crouching over Arif, he felt for the servant's pulse.

"A steady pulse. Good," Damon announced, sitting back on his heels and gesturing to the open window. "Looks like that severed part was thrown through the broken window. It hit Arif on the head, knocking him out. Get me a cold cloth and I'll try to revive him."

As I turned to do Damon's bidding, I tossed over my shoulder, "It was probably meant for me. What I'd like to know is how the person knew I was here."

"Must be you're being followed."

Damon pointed to the gory object on the floor. The stained piece of paper was still attached. I averted my eyes while he removed the note and glanced at it. When he was done he stuffed it in his pocket. I didn't know how to interpret his expression.

"Are you planning on showing me that?" I asked.

"Later."

I wanted to know now, but we had to take care of Arif. I handed Damon a wet kitchen towel with ice cubes folded into it. He applied the makeshift compress to Arif's forehead and in seconds the East Indian's eyes fluttered open. *"Duk cha…"*

"Bad," I translated. I'd been stuck in the hotel

with time on my hands and pretty much memorized the phrase book. "Bad headache is probably what he means."

"I'm impressed, Phe."

The servant was slowly coming to. He shook his head as if to clear it and tried to sit up. Damon pressed him back to the floor and in more lucid tones Arif said, "Madame's tea, I must get it."

Damon applied the compress against the man's forehead. "You're not getting anything right now, pal." To me, he said, "Go find Madame Wong and let her know her man will be okay. He might need a doctor's attention but at the very least he should rest."

Relieved it was nothing more serious than perhaps a bad concussion, I went off to find Althea and Madeline. They were seated on one of the ornate damask couches in the living room. Madeline's color was slowly returning to her face but I could tell she was badly shaken.

"Arif isn't seriously injured," I announced. "He had the wind knocked out of him, that's all, and he has a nasty bruise to his head. You may want to get a doctor."

Madeline rubbed the spot where her heart should be. "This is like one of your horror movies. I have never experienced such a thing. If Arif needs a doctor I shall take him to the hospital in town."

"We'll take him to the hospital," I said. "You've already had enough to deal with."

"No, no. I'll take him. You came to tea and you should have it. After I check on Arif I'll decide what to do."

Madeline was almost back to her old bossy self. She sailed off, leaving me to explain to Althea what had occurred. I still didn't know what the note said, but I knew that goat's foot had been meant for me.

Althea grimaced. "Phoenix, you can't just ignore what's been happening. Things are escalating and getting crazier. You should get the police involved."

"I'm not going to give anyone the satisfaction of thinking they're scaring me. I mean to find out who's at the bottom of this."

Madeline was back, Damon in tow. Althea and I waited to hear what she was about to say.

"Arif does not want to go to the hospital. I sent him off to his quarters to rest. We'll have our tea and catch up. My driver will get you back to your hotel before curfew."

Not one mention of a goat's foot. She acted as if it had never happened. I wondered how Damon had disposed of the hoof. I'd ask him later.

For the next hour while Madeline poured tea and served finger sandwiches, tarts and delicious iced cakes, she kept up a running commentary about what a sorry state of affairs the Tibetan government was in.

She bemoaned the continued destruction of Tibetan cultural and religious monuments which occurred after the Chinese Red Guards arrived.

It was fascinating to me to hear a Chinese from Hong Kong speak so poorly of her own. Tibet was Madeline's adopted home. Her recounting of the atrocities heaped on the Tibetans, the beatings, tortures and jailings for expressing a political opinion, got my ire up.

Madeline took me aside when we were in the kitchen, where I was helping her put away the leftovers. She wagged a long painted nail at me. "I want you to be careful. This government is corrupt and the members of the PSB are more likely than not in the pockets of one or another of the officials. There are those who feel inadequate because a foreigner was brought in to restore what they think an artisan monk can do and for a cheaper price."

"Thank you for the warning. I'm thrilled to have been selected to restore such a valued piece of art," I said. "This is still a job to me and afterward I'll be going home. No one need worry about me establishing permanent residency here."

"They do not see it that way. I'll protect you

as best as I can. My contacts are far-reaching but this is still not considered my home and I am technically not one of them."

Madeline stopped to scribble something on a notepad. She folded the paper into my palm.

"You have my house phone. Now you have this. You are to use this number if you are ever in trouble. Feel safe to leave a message with whoever answers. They can be trusted."

I thanked her and shoved the note in the pocket of my pants. Hopefully I would never need to use the number.

"I must get you home before it grows dark," Madeline said, linking an arm through mine. "Your young man must be wondering what we're up to. He is charming and very fond of you."

"He is not my young man," I quickly corrected. "And definitely not fond of me."

She smiled enigmatically. "It is not time for him to show you just how much. You are not ready. After he proves himself, maybe."

What did she see that I didn't see? Damon and I were long over. Discretion being the better part of valor, I smiled and followed Madeline out to the courtyard where Althea and Damon were chatting. White-tipped mountaintops rimmed the twelve-foot brick wall and created a picturesque halo. The setting created a peaceful tranquility. It made me vow to spend more time outdoors. I would not, and could not, let a stalker inhibit my movements.

Eventually we said our goodbyes and climbed back into the Mercedes. Despite the earlier episode, I was glad I had come. Madeline's home felt like a haven to me.

She peered through the open window. "I'll call Xiong Jing first thing tomorrow and see what's holding the project up. *Tashi deleh*," she said, waving us off.

"Good luck," I translated.

I couldn't wait to get back to the hotel. Damon and I needed to talk. I wanted to read the note that was meant for me, and I didn't feel comfortable doing so in front of Althea. I must be onto something or why would I be a threat?

"I want to know what's in that note," I demanded, the moment Althea had gone upstairs to her room, leaving Damon and I alone.

"Why be a masochist? You already know what it says. Someone's trying to scare you so that you'll pack up and leave."

"Stop trying to protect me, just hand it over." I held out my hand.

The side of Damon's mouth tilted upward in a familiar smirk. His need to manage me, shield me from God knew what, was one of the things that had irked me. I did not need a caretaker to make decisions for me. I was not and would never be anyone's little woman.

"Okay, Phe. I'm walking you up to your room and checking things out."

"Suit yourself."

Secretly I felt relieved. The thought of visitors, the four-legged kind, didn't sit well with me.

Inside, I made sure to keep him as far away from my bed as possible. No point in giving him ideas.

"The note," I insisted, my hand still held out.

"I'd hoped you'd forgotten about it."

He was stalling, trying to spare me from reading the ugly message. Kind of him but totally unnecessary.

My hand remained out. "It's me they're after," I said. "I should know what I'm up against."

Reluctantly, Damon reached into his jeans pocket and extracted the bloodstained note. "It's ugly," he warned, slipping it into my open palm.

I braced myself for the worst. The wording was neither original nor subtle.

Yankee woman go home. To stay means doing so at your own risk. Mutilating a goat is only one example of what we can do.

This wasn't just some local hood trying to scare me. I suspected my enemy had far-reaching contacts with some pull.

Damon took the note back. His gaze remained on my face. "'We' would imply there's more than one person behind this. Who were the local candidates for the job, do you know? Finding out might be a good place to start."

"I could call Madeline Wong and ask her. She seems to know everything."

Damon swallowed his puff pastry and helped himself to another hors d'oeuvre.

"I've already figured out she helped you to get the job."

"Yes, she was instrumental. Sometimes it helps to cash in on your connections. When I first heard about the opportunity I sent Madeline an e-mail. She'd always said if I needed her to pull strings on my behalf she would, and she came through."

"In the process she upset the person who thought they had the job," Damon managed through a full mouth.

"Why go to those lengths? Why try to harm me?"

"You're allowing your Western thought process to kick in."

Damon plopped down on my bed and stretched out.

"I am Western," I reminded him.

"You don't need to save face."

"Sometimes I do. Take for example Maitreya. Restoring that statue is important to me."

Damon patted the spot next to him. "Pour us some wine and let's brainstorm together."

He was taking control. Nevertheless, I poured the wine, reasoning that both he and I could use something to help us chill. In the back of my mind I knew that mixing alcohol with Damon was not good.

Gingerly I sat down. "What are you thinking?"

"I'm thinking Madeline Wong may have stepped on a few toes when she wangled this job for you. High-profile restoration projects are political and the PR it brings can only increase business. You'll be highly sought after afterward."

"And so will you," I added.

"Lie down and make yourself comfortable, Phe. Okay, so let's say the person who wants you out of the way is high up in the government…"

"What are you thinking?"

"The government building was bombed?"

"And you're thinking someone hired the pickpocket on the plane, and that he was probably after my documents. I wouldn't have been able to get into the country without a passport, visa and return ticket."

Maybe Damon had something after all.

Damon's fingers kneaded my lower back. "Be careful, Phe. Watch yourself."

He sat up and, using his nose, nuzzled my back.

"I will be careful. I'm nothing if not careful."

"It could very well be organized crime," Damon added.

I hadn't thought of that.

"And you're thinking this is just the beginning. That someone would kill me and think nothing of it."

"They've been trying their damnedest."

It was a sobering thought that someone would go so far as murder. It made me not want to be alone. It made me wonder what it would be like to allow Damon to protect me.

"You've frustrated them, Phe. You're not taking these warnings seriously. You had to know there would be consequences."

"I'm not backing off," I said with more gusto than I actually felt. "I need to get my hands on that statue."

"And if it's a fake?"

"That's a chance I'll have to take. On the other hand, if it's Bhaisajyaguru, and not Maitreya, then I am closer to clearing my father's name. It's the reason he lost his job. It's why he became depressed. I need to prove to the world that my father is not a bad man. And I need to help get him off a path of destruction."

Damon's fingers continued to knead my flesh. "I've always loved that about you," he whispered. "You'll go out of your way to fight an injustice."

Loved? No, Damon did not love me. Never. Ever. If he had, he would never have made me choose between our relationship and a job that would launch my career.

Best to stick to a safe subject.

"I'd do just about anything to have my old father back again," I said.

"I'd do just about anything to have you back," Damon whispered ever so softly. If I hadn't been carefully listening I would have missed it.

My eyes misted over. Then he kissed me and the years fell away. I was twenty years old and back in Florence again, insanely in love with a man that was my everything.

Chapter 6

Finally, we were here, settled in at our quarters at the Deprung Monastery. The call had come from Xiong Jing. I could only assume I had Madame Wong to thank for making this happen.

"Can your crew be ready to leave within the hour?" he'd asked.

I'd assured him we could. We'd already been delayed five days and if I had to pack them up myself, I was making this move happen. Plus, being in a hotel with Damon with time on my hands was proving to be dangerous. Lucky for me, I'd come to my senses last evening before we got busy. That kiss was enough. Denying my aching body, I'd practically pushed him from the room.

A minivan had picked us up to take us to the monastery. We'd then been met by a monk and taken to a convent that would be our home for the next few weeks. The cells that we moved into were by no means fancy but they were functional. A communal bathroom was located down a long hallway.

I made a quick check of my new accommodations to make sure there weren't any nasty surprises. Call me paranoid but after what I'd been through I wasn't taking chances.

Slowly, I began unpacking. I placed my meager wardrobe in the wooden closet provided, and a photo of my family taken at Christmas two years before on top of the chest of drawers. We'd all looked so happy back then.

I'd been considering going for a run but changed my mind. I set off to explore my new home.

My thought was to wander around while I was still incognito and take photos. Damon, Althea and I were to meet with Xiong Jing within the hour, so there wasn't much time to waste.

I'd acquired a map from the concierge. Following a pathway, I headed for the center of the monastery. On the way in I'd spotted the Main Assembly Hall, known as Tshomchen and the four tantric colleges.

The Buddhas inside were what interested me. In particular I wanted to see "The Gilded Buddha," and Shakyamuni, considered the founder of Buddhism. Both were enshrined on the second floor of the Main Assembly Hall. I was dying to get a good look at the bronze version of the eight-year-old Maitreya, enshrined in a smaller hall.

I planned on committing every minor detail of Maitreya's construction to memory. And if I could, I would take many pictures. The miniversion of Maitreya was a direct replica of the larger more valuable idol, or so I'd been told.

Footsteps behind me caused me to pause, but every time I looked around there was no one behind me. The gardeners and laborers working the grounds so far hadn't even glanced my way. They probably weren't particularly interested in a foreigner.

I'd stopped to examine a particularly scary-looking Buddha, a protector statue, guarding the more valuable Buddhas inside, when I sensed the presence again.

More and more people filed by. Deprung was turning out to be a popular destination. I watched money surreptitiously change hands with employees in exchange for snapshots of an artifact or other valuable piece.

I hustled toward the area knowing full well that I was being observed and might even be falling in with the plan. He or she might have a weapon. It was a chance I was willing to take. I was bound and determined to find out who wanted me out of the way and why.

Almost two feet away I heard the sound of labored breathing. A speck of saffron billowed from behind the post. I pretended to change my mind and made an abrupt U-turn. An audible sigh of relief—or was it exasperation?—floated my way. I continued to walk, feigning interest in another idol which had captured my attention. Surreptitiously I glanced at my watch. After a few minutes I doubled back, coming at the person from the other direction.

I could see him clearly behind the column. He was half standing, half crouching, peering in the direction that I'd initially headed. On tiptoe I crept up on him and clamped a hand on his shoulder, spinning him around.

"What do you want from me?" I asked. My mouth opened wide then snapped shut. I was not prepared for the deformed face that greeted me with the half-closed lid and the eye missing from its socket. Nor was I prepared for the toothless mouth that rounded itself into an O.

I repeated myself.

This time my words were greeted by a wide smile and hand signals that I first interpreted as an inability to speak English.

My stalker continued to make convoluted hand signals, pointing this way and that. It finally struck me that he'd been following me because he thought I might be interested in a tour of the monastery. What a fool I was. I should be ashamed for suspecting an innocent monk who was just trying to be hospitable.

Reaching into the pocket of my cargo pants, I found a notepad, retrieved it and scribbled my name.

"Phoenix," I said, shoving it at him, pointing to myself and then at the note. "Phoenix," I repeated.

His mouth made another round O then became an upturned C. He signaled for me to hand over the pad and I did. He scribbled something in Tibetan. I shook my head. Then he wrote one word, *Tashi,* and gestured to his mouth, wiggling his forefinger back and forth.

"Tashi?" I repeated.

"Ngah Tashi yin," he wrote.

It was one of the first phrases I'd learned in the

Tibetan-English dictionary. The monk was telling me his name.

"*Ngah Phoenix yin,*" I said, introducing myself.

The finger went to Tashi's mouth then wiggled back and forth again.

I finally got it. He was deaf.

"You do not speak," I scribbled, taking the pad back and holding it up in front of him.

He nodded. We were beginning to communicate.

Another hand motion indicated his interest in accompanying me into the assembly hall. I was starting to view this as an adventure with some intriguing possibilities. Not everyone had a monk as their personal escort.

I followed him upstairs of the main assembly hall and managed to take a few pictures of the scriptures that were preserved. Then I motioned I wanted to go to the smaller hall and found to my surprise a number of people worshipping what looked to be a conch shell enshrined in front of the young Maitreya.

My puzzled look made Tashi point a bent finger at a bronze plaque recapping the history. The shell was supposedly used by Sakyamuni, founder of Buddhism, then afterward hidden at Mount Gambo. Tsong Khapa discovered it there and gave it to his disciple as a monastery treasure. It very well could be a fable, but each culture had their legends and this one in particular fascinated me.

My competitive spirit ignited, I was now even more determined to brush up on my history. If for no other reason than to throw it in Damon's face that even though he'd converted to Buddhism, he didn't have a thing over me.

I managed another set of discreet photographs of the junior Maitreya while my guide gaped. He was fascinated by my digital camera, which was a little bigger than a credit card, but not by much.

Outside, I showed him the images I'd captured. Like a little boy he clapped his hands gleefully, pointed to his chest and back at me. It dawned on me he wanted a photograph of us together.

I flagged down a couple of backpacking tourists, guessing by the Union Jacks on the front of their T-shirts, they were British. They graciously agreed to take photos of me and Tashi and asked to have the favor returned. Tashi had become a star. My new monk friend seemed delighted by the attention and was hamming it up.

After the photo-taking, we exchanged a few pleasantries and moved on. Tashi now began making animated gestures with his hands. His expression soon matched his outrageous gesticulations. I finally figured out that he was inviting me to have tea with him at his quarters.

Although it was a thoughtful and kind gesture, my caution buttons lit up. About an hour ago the monk had been following me, and now we'd become instant friends. Besides, I had someplace to be. Now, how to politely decline?

I scribbled a note saying, "Thank you, maybe some other time." Then I put my hands together as if praying and nodded my head. He nodded an acknowledgment back. It occurred to me that maybe he deserved and even expected some yuan for the guided tour. But when I tried to pass him money, his good eye ticked, and, horrified, he backed away from me.

To make my meeting I'd have to jog. The courtyard where we were meeting Xiong Jing was close to our sleeping quarters and well away from the tourist haunts. At one point it must have been where the monks met to pray. Now it was simply a charming place to spend your time and meditate.

Hoping that Tashi would understand, I gestured that I needed to go. He seemed sad but I was running late and I had no time for reassurances. I raced off.

Damon, Xiong Jing and Althea were standing round in a circle in front of one of the temples when I arrived. I glanced at my watch. I was only about five minutes late but I still felt guilty. I wasn't setting much of an example.

"You're late," Damon pointed out as if I didn't know it.

"Sorry. I was in the midst of a conversation with one of the monks and got carried away."

Xiong Jing wore his impassive expression. With the exception of a few phone calls to inquire about my well-being, and a feeble attempt to update me on the status of the project, contact with him had been minimal.

All eyes were on me now.

"You are unpacked and settled?" Xiong Jing asked, trying for graciousness.

"Yes, and raring to go to work." I smiled brightly.

There was no answering smile.

"That is a good thing. There is much to do."

It sounded like a prelude to another stall. "Is there a particular building we'll be working out of?" I asked.

"But of course. The statue remains in its crate. Security guards watch it day and night."

"Then we will begin work in the morning at seven o'clock sharp."

"I am afraid not. Our historical preservation society wants to meet with you first. They want to discuss with you the plans for restoration. It is important that our Maitreya is restored to its former glory and as authentically as possible."

A new twist. "How come I haven't heard about this historical preservation organization before?" I asked.

Xiong Jing shrugged. "Perhaps they saw no point in discussion before now."

"When will this meeting take place?"

Another shrug followed. "When they have time to gather."

"But that could be weeks. We are on a tight deadline."

"Do not fret. You are being paid for your time here. If I were you, I'd relax and enjoy myself."

I exhaled an openmouthed breath. Another delay. Was there no end?

Chapter 7

My thoughts returned to Damon. I would make sure to tell him Althea was joining us, so he didn't misinterpret my dinner invitation.

As I walked through the grounds, I remembered the shared kiss. That kiss had awakened something inside of me that I'd been determined to ignore. I tried to shake it off.

The area where our sleeping quarters were was set back from the main thoroughfare. I wound my way through several crumbling pathways made darker by the absence of direct sunlight. The quiet was eerie. All I could hear was my own breathing. I'd always relied on my instincts and every sense went on alert.

Darting a quick glance behind me, I hurried up the three front steps of the convent, scowling at the protecting Buddhas guarding the entrance. So far I hadn't encountered a living soul. I entered the common area and walked by the uncomfortable chairs that served as seating. Then I headed to the right, wandering down a long, dark hallway.

I didn't exactly feel comfortable arriving at his cell unannounced, so I tried making noises to announce my arrival. I thudded my heels on the stone floor and ran my hands along the walls. Knocking on the door, I stood and cupped my hands around my mouth, calling, "Damon! Where are you?"

No answer.

"Damon!" I shouted even louder now, growing more concerned as the seconds ticked by.

All of a sudden a hand clamped over my mouth, cutting off my oxygen. The other hand gripped my braid, jerking my neck back. I was practically yanked off my feet and dragged down the hallway. I was flung into a dimly lit cell and the door slammed behind me. There was nothing to break my fall except the arms I held out and my blistered palms. A sharp pain ricocheted through my body then everything around me went black.

I awoke cold and numb. My limbs felt stiff and my cheek and arm stung where I must have bruised them.

Through my fog I heard my name being called. I was sure of it. *Althea?*

I heard my name again, this time louder.

"Phoenix! Where are you?"

I made myself move, even tried to get to my feet but the pain was excruciating. I sank back onto my butt and dragged myself in the total darkness to where I thought the door might be. Using the heels of my ankle boots, I kicked out, thudding my soles against a wooden surface.

"Althea!" I shouted as loudly as I could.

"Phe, Phoenix! Yell if you can hear us."

A man's voice, probably Damon's. Couldn't they hear me?

"Phoenix, if you're in here, answer."

"I'm here. I'm here!" I shouted as loudly as I could. Using my heels, I pounded against wood.

Were those footsteps I heard coming closer? Summoning all of my strength, I tried standing up. My body ached but nothing seemed broken. I rose to my feet slowly and anchored myself against a wall, cautiously edging around the periphery of the room, hoping to locate the door and a handle.

All the while I kept shouting, "Althea! Damon! I'm in here."

The footsteps stopped. It seemed quiet, too quiet.

Then my hands located a knob. I twisted and turned but the door refused to budge. Forgetting about the pain racking my body, I hurled myself against the door. Not once or twice, but until the door shook and I thought it might splinter.

The footsteps started up again, quicker, coming directly toward me. A male voice, so close. "She's in there. Stay back."

The door heaved, shook, rattled, groaned and splintered open. I moved back and placed an arm over my eyes. When I opened them, Althea and Damon were standing before me.

"Oh, my God, Phoenix, what happened?" Althea asked, her hand covering her mouth.

I must have looked pretty bad, because Damon wrapped a hand around my forearm, anchoring me. "Steady."

"I have a first-aid kit in my room," Damon said, calm as ever. "Let's get these bruises cleaned up. From now on no one goes anywhere unless they're in pairs. Hear me?"

Ignoring the soreness that was settling in, I managed to make my legs move as he and Althea half carried, half walked me down the hallway.

Inside Damon's cell I was seated on a hard wooden chair. I noticed the altar set up in the corner and tried to imagine him chanting there. It seemed so out of character for the Damon I remembered, who'd believed he was invincible and needed no one, to worship there.

He set to work cleaning my bruised face, and arms, and applying antiseptic to my blistered palms. Althea had gone off to make tea. Damon squatted down. "Roll up your pant legs," he ordered.

"I can take care of my own bruises," I muttered grumpily.

"No, you can't."

He sat back on his haunches, his gray eyes a chilling shade of flint. While he chided me gently, he held on to my ankle. "I can't ever let you out of my sight, Phe. Whenever I do, you manage to get into trouble."

Who did he think he was, my father?

"I came to find you to go to dinner," I snapped. "Maybe I shouldn't have." It was a childish outburst but it did give me satisfaction lashing out at him. I was angry at myself for walking into a trap and having to rely on Damon to rescue me.

"Yes, Althea mentioned you were looking for me. I ran into her and we both waited for you to come back. When an hour passed we figured something was wrong."

The old resentment flared up again. I remembered a time when he answered for me and attempted to make decisions that were mine alone to make.

Althea was back carrying three mugs on a tray. Her gaze flickered down to where Damon held my ankle. She maintained a poker face and set down the tray, handing me my mug before picking up her own.

Damon rolled up my pant legs and began swabbing at my bruises.

"Dinner on the town appears to be out now," he said affably. "We have a curfew to abide by. Maybe we could see if the dining hall is still open."

We'd been introduced to the dining area earlier by Ven, the monk put in charge of us. Its Spartan-like atmosphere was not conducive to leisurely meals. Food was served cafeteria style and youthful monks served in various capacities, anything from cook to busboy and general cleaner-upper. The food laid out in warming trays was simple but plentiful. I'd hoped to sample the salted butter tea, yogurt, Tibetan noodles and dumplings. I'd even thought of trying the mutton, but the blood, liver sausages and the yak tongue were definitely off-limits.

My rumbling stomach indicated I was starving.

"I could use something to eat," I announced.

"While we eat we can figure out a plan for tomorrow. Meeting with Xiong Jing was a waste anyway. His whole speech about the historical preservation society was just another delaying tactic. Makes you wonder, doesn't it?"

"Yes, it does," Althea responded. "I'm not sure I like him, plus, his stalling is getting old. I'm deeply concerned about these attempts on your life. It wouldn't hurt to get familiar with the layout of the monastery, at least with the area where we're expected to work."

I couldn't agree more.

Damon continued swabbing at my smarting wounds. "I'm doing the best that I can," he announced.

I thanked him grudgingly. He had, after all, rescued me. Then I said, "I'd like to take a look at Maitreya, tomorrow. We shouldn't need the historical preservation society's permission to do that. Ouch! Easy."

The peroxide had settled into a particularly brutal wound.

"Why don't you call Madame Wong again and have her pull some strings," Althea suggested. "She might very well be on the board of this society. The woman does have contacts in all the right places."

Damon stood up and set down the bottle of

peroxide. "Think you can navigate the outdoors?" he asked, offering me an arm.

If it meant dragging myself down a pathway on my butt, I would do so rather than taking his arm. "I can manage," I huffed, awkwardly stumbling toward the door. Feeling bad for the attitude, I turned back and thanked him.

A silent Althea observed the interaction between the two of us. She brought up the rear as we wove our way through more courtyards and archways. After a few wrong turns we found the dining hall.

When we entered the dining area, a number of silent monks sat around tables drinking what looked to be barley broth from bowls. They didn't seem particularly interested in our arrival and barely looked at us.

Damon secured a table at the front of the hall. "Sit," he said, waving us into the chairs. "I'll get you whatever you need."

I gratefully sank into the seat. "I'll have whatever they're having," I said, my gesture taking in the monks and their simple fare. "Maybe I'll try a side dish of noodles as well."

"You've got it." Damon hurried off.

"Aren't you going to get yourself something to eat?" I asked Althea, who remained with me.

"After Damon gets back."

She'd always been loyal and supportive. When you're the only two African-American women at an art center in Florence, you tend to become tight. Our bond had been almost instantaneous.

"How long was I missing?" I asked.

"I got worried when you weren't back in half an hour. Then Damon showed up and we waited together another half an hour. All in all, a little over an hour."

Damon was back, bearing a tray of assorted foods, enough to feed a small army. He set the tray down and removed dishes and utensils, handing them to us. A monk who looked as if he was barely in his teens poured water from a pitcher. We thanked him and he nodded solemnly.

"Okay, so what's the plan for tomorrow?" Damon asked after we began to eat.

"I'm going to do some nosing around," I answered. "I'd like to find that gardener who dug up the crate with Maitreya. And I'd like to find the building where the statue is kept. It would be nice to see our work site."

"What about Madame Wong?" Althea prodded. "I thought we were enlisting her help with this preservation society or whatever it's called?"

I nodded. Trust Althea to keep me focused. "In the morning I'll call her."

"Phe, I'm worried," Damon admitted, his fingers making a rat-a-tat noise against the wooden surface of the table. "About you. This whole thing. We have a deadline to meet yet nothing seems to get moving. It's been one disaster after another. It's as if this project is doomed."

"I'm surprised to hear you say that. You're always so positive."

We'd finished our meal and were the only people in the place, except for the monks cleaning up.

"How do we pay for this?" I asked.

"I already did," Damon answered. "What say we turn in early, rest up, and get an early start tomorrow? By the way, I'll be sleeping with you tonight."

"What?"

Althea and I exchanged incredulous looks.

"You heard me," Damon said as calm as ever. "No way am I leaving you alone."

Chapter 8

True to his word and although I tried to dissuade him, Damon maintained a watchful position in a sleeping bag at the foot of my bed. Having him there did not make it easy to fall asleep. I found myself fantasizing, remembering a time when he was an extension of me, and we snuggled in the same bed, spooning.

"Phe, are you awake?" Damon mumbled from his place south of me.

"Yes, I'm awake. What's up?" I grumbled.

He rustled around in his sleeping bag, presumably sitting up. "Remember the time we went backpacking through the Italian wine country and how much wine we drank?"

I grunted. What I remembered was us making love, every opportunity we could, and in some mighty uncomfortable places at that. Why did he pick now, of all times, when I was vulnerable, to bring this up? .

That summer had been especially memorable for me. I'd fallen in love with him, hopelessly and completely. Our semester had ended and we'd needed a break to decompress. Neither of us wanted to go home to the United States so we'd decided to stay on in Europe and explore.

We'd thrown a few items into backpacks and decided to take off. Armed with maps and the usual assortment of tourist pamphlets, we'd hopped a train and gotten off whenever and wherever we felt the notion. At times we pointed a finger to a place, liking the sound of its name, and so another adventure would begin.

Days were spent exploring the countryside, popping in at one vineyard or another. We'd drink wine and chat up the locals, who always were remarkably fluent in English as most Europeans tended to be. At night, after a simple, filling dinner, and more wine, we'd book into a youth hostel or a cheap inn, and make love as if there was no tomorrow.

"Those were good times," Damon said in a deeply seductive voice I was trying my best to ignore. "I miss them."

I was not about to go there. "We were young and in love. Idealists," I responded, attempting to ground him.

"We had dreams. And we had each other."

I didn't want to hear this. The tenor of the conversation was getting much too personal. There was no point in rehashing what could have been.

When it was time to support me, Damon had shown his true colors. His declarations of love had gone quickly out the window when I chose my career over him.

During this journey down memory lane, Damon had managed to crawl out of his sleeping bag. He was now perched on the edge of my bed.

A hand fluttered across my shoulder blade. I froze. "Phe, don't you miss us?"

"There hasn't been an *us* for quite some time," I said, infusing sleep in my voice, hoping he would leave it at that.

"You gave us up."

"No, you did."

He was rubbing my back now. The warmth of his palms seeping into my skin, easing the chill that two blankets couldn't keep away.

"The first time I spotted you," Damon reminisced, "I thought you were a model. You didn't look a thing like the other students. Most couldn't care less about their appearance."

"I didn't care, either. I wore carpenter pants and baggy T-shirts like the other kids. My idea of dressing up was putting on a clean oxford shirt."

"And you looked lovely. It didn't really matter what you wore." Damon's fingers kneaded away at my shoulders. They moved upward to make circles at my nape. "You were exotic and smart, and I wanted you."

The tension eased a bit. Damon's voice held me spellbound. I might just be able to fall asleep after all.

His warm breath blew against my chilled flesh. I went on alert, stiffening.

"What are you doing?" I asked.

"Trying to get you to relax."

A feather-soft kiss seared my skin.

"Stop it, Damon."

His hands were on my nape again, kneading, soothing.

"You're wound as tight as a spring."

I hated to admit it, but Damon's massaging hands on my back felt wonderful. My entire body was beginning to tingle and buzz.

"Take off your clothes."

"What?"

"You heard me."

I was no longer angry but resigned to the inevitable. I was his, totally and completely.

"You take them off," I whispered.

I drifted on a cloud. Damon began tugging off my pants. He pulled my sweatshirt over my head. Soon I lay there without a stitch on, listening to rustling as he disrobed.

My body was already afire, my nerve endings wired. Damon's hands soothed my flesh. He blew warm puffs of air on my body.

"Phe," he whispered. "I should stop. I'm being selfish. You have scrapes and bruises all over your body, they must hurt."

"Not anymore."

I was way beyond feeling pain. It was about pleasure now.

The only thing I thought of was Damon's warm soothing hands on my breasts, kneading away until my nipples went taut. His rough palm grazing my stomach and the heat spiraling downward to settle in my throbbing center. If he kept it up I would implode.

One night, I reasoned. Just one night of loving. Tomorrow it would be back to business.

Damon's body settled on me. His muscles rippled under my hand and his musky animal scent filled my nostrils. He spoke softly in Spanglish.

"*Querida…mi amor…*touch me. Yes, *aqui*. Here."

And I touched him, responding to his directions, cupping his buttocks and finding all the secret places that turned him on.

I knew exactly when he was ready and opened up to him. He shielded himself then entered me and waited for me to wrap my ankles around his. I arched my back. His long slow strokes left me quaking. My nails ripped into his back.

Damon nipped the sides of my neck. I held firm, keeping him stationary. He broke free, entering me again, this time with intensity. We'd always liked things a little rough. Not rough enough to hurt, but enough to let each other know we were equally passionately involved.

He began to spasm. I exploded, matching him shudder for shudder. Release felt good. Afterward we lay with our limbs intertwined, Damon's soft snores in my ears. We'd always been good together.

Grabbing a handful of his hair, I tugged on it.

"You need to get back into your sleeping bag," I snapped.

"Your warmth was short-lived," he grumbled, cocky as ever. Damon rolled off me and scrambled to find his clothing.

"Can you blame me? You still fall asleep right after, and snore."

"And you still make that little clicking sound at the back of your throat when you climax."

I didn't bother answering. Didn't want him reminding me. He climbed back into his sleeping bag and in a short time the snoring started.

I twisted and turned and couldn't fall asleep. What little sleep I did get was filled with horrendous nightmares.

Someone was shaking me. "Phe, it's time to get up. Xiong Jing is here. He wants to meet with us at breakfast. He's waiting at the dining hall."

Groggy, I struggled from bed, gathered clean underwear and a sweatshirt, and made my way down the hall to the communal bathroom. Damon followed. Determined to put last night out of my mind, I relieved myself. Afterward, I splashed water on my face, cleaned up a bit and braided my hair. Then I changed underwear, stepped back into the pants I had slept in and threw on a sweatshirt.

When I walked out, Damon's hair was wet and slicked back. He looked as though he was fresh out of the shower and seemed very relaxed.

"Ready?" he asked.

"Ready," I answered. "Shall we pop by Althea's cell and pick her up?"

"She's already over at the dining hall."

That meant it was just him.

"How did you sleep?" he asked.

"Lousy. I kept having these dreams that the statue had been stolen and no one wanted to tell us."

"I was up all night, too," Damon admitted, although he hardly looked fatigued.

When we entered the hall, Althea and Xiong Jing seemed to be in deep discussion.

"Good morning," I said, joining them.

Xiong Jing got to his feet, greeting me. Despite the thick accent and the Asian outward appearance, he was very Westernized.

"Good morning. I trust you slept well?"

"She didn't," Damon interjected and proceeded to explain to the project manager that I had been attacked and locked into a vacant cell.

"That is most upsetting. Did you contact the police?" Xiong Jing asked.

Damon and I exchanged looks. Why bother answering? We both thought they were useless. Suddenly Damon looked at his watch, said to wait for him, and disappeared.

"What's the plan for today?" I asked. "When can we meet with this historical preservation society?"

"That I will have to get back to you on."

I was starting to get irritated and I am sure it

showed. Plus my bruises stung and my limbs felt heavy.

"Will you take us to the place where the idol is being kept?" I asked. "We'd like to see the conditions we'll be working under. Wouldn't we, team?" I looked to the others for confirmation. They nodded.

Xiong Jing glanced at his watch. "Not today. Maybe tomorrow. I have a meeting with Liu Bangfu in less than an hour. I will need to give him an update on what has happened."

"Shouldn't we be included in this meeting? Timelines are going to need to be changed," Althea offered, speaking up at last.

"I shall talk to the minister about setting up a separate meeting. He is a bit preoccupied these days. His wife has taken ill, and the doctors are unable to diagnose or properly treat the ailment."

This was a new one. My natural compassion kicked in but the minister's ignoring of us bordered on being downright rude.

"I'm sorry to hear that," I said. "Why don't you tell us where the statue is? We'll walk over to the area and see if there's something we can help with."

Xiong Jing seemed to hesitate. We all stared at him. Finally he said, "Do you have the map of the monastery I gave you yesterday?"

Althea waved a folded-up map she'd taken from her pocket. "I do."

The project manager drew some lines and arrows up and down several alleyways, and across a half-dozen courtyards. He then traced a path uphill before making a large red X on an ancient doorway. "It might be a bit difficult to get there. A finding of such importance has to be kept off the beaten track. I must go now. I will be in touch soon."

Nodding in our direction, he left.

"What do we do now?" Althea asked. "We've still got well over an hour to spare."

"Try to find the place housing Maitreya."

"But what about Damon? We promised to meet him and we were to go together."

"And we will," I answered, unfolding the map and pointing out a path. "Let's take a right through that alleyway and then hang left."

"But, Phoenix, that area looks pretty isolated. Shouldn't we at least wait for Damon? Given what's been going on, I'd feel better if we had a man along."

I narrowed my eyes, hoping she would get the message. "And what will Damon do that I can't do? I don't believe he has a black belt in karate-jitsu."

"Mea culpa," Althea responded, pretending to

be awed. "That's right, you do, but it didn't seem to help you last evening. Did it?"

"Don't remind me."

We continued on our way, darting glances at the map as we went along. Every now and then I thought I heard the sound of gravel underfoot or a twig snap. Althea put voice to our suspicions.

"I think we're being followed," she said in a tight little voice.

"I think you might be right." I stopped abruptly and looked around. No sign of anyone and not a sound. We started off again, not exchanging a word but listening intently. A long, dark alleyway lay ahead. A glance at our map indicated it ended at a debating courtyard, a place where monks gathered in animated groups to practice highly stylized debating skills.

"Let's not risk it, Phoenix," Althea pleaded. "Can't we stick to a more populated area?"

I heard the rustle of fabric and turned around. A splash of saffron disappeared behind an archway. I motioned to Althea to walk ahead of me and stood there dead still, waiting.

Five minutes went by, before Tashi, my monk friend, with his winning smile that some might call gruesome, showed his face.

Chapter 9

He bowed. I bowed back. Tashi made no bones about being happy to see me. I signaled it was safe to come closer. He slid a notebook from under his robe and approached. He began writing. "Where are you going? Can I come with you?"

I took the notebook from him and wrote back. "I am trying to find the statue that was found in the garden."

The notebook exchanged hands again. "I can take you."

I decided to take him up on his offer. Having him along would make things so much easier. I wouldn't have to rely on a map. I pointed to Althea, who was walking slowly ahead, stopping every few steps while pretending to admire the architecture. I mimicked that we were together.

Tashi gave a slight nod but I could tell he wasn't that comfortable about having Althea along.

"Althea," I called. "Wait up."

She stood perfectly still, watching Tashi fall in step beside me. Together we approached her.

Althea remained expressionless when I used Tashi's notebook and made introductions, explaining that she and I were longtime friends and she could be trusted. He immediately relaxed and even offered up another gruesome smile.

Suddenly he darted up a darkened stairwell, beckoning us to follow. Althea and I exchanged looks before following him. What if it was some kind of trap?

The staircase led onto an open roof revealing a sweeping view of the Kyichu Valley. This panoramic vista almost took my breath away. I was literally on the roof of the world; in Tibet, a place I had dreamed of. Guttural sounds came from Tashi's throat as he pointed out the pilgrim's circuit running in a clockwise manner and the miniature people darting in and out of buildings.

We needed to move on. I pointed to the stairwell. Althea and I headed toward it. Tashi trailed us. A brisk ten-minute walk followed through another series of alleys, courtyards, and up steep steps. It finally led to buildings that appeared to be abandoned. Uniformed officers, with their guns trained on us, seemed a clear indication we were on the right track.

One of them, a gaunt, balding man, barked something in Chinese. Tashi quickly scribbled on his paper. "He says the area is restricted. You need credentials to get in."

I fumbled in my pants pocket for the identification I carried. Xiong Jing had also gotten us a badge stating Resident Artists.

The policeman took a cursory look at Althea's and my credentials. He made a shooing noise at Tashi and waved his hand, dismissing him. The monk sped off, apparently afraid of the grim-looking man waving the machine gun. I motioned to the policeman Althea and I needed to enter.

"Work has not yet begun," he said in surprisingly good English.

"I need to see the idol I'll be working on." I produced my camera and shook it at him. "Mr. Bangfu says I can take pictures."

The minister's name seemed to work magic. The officer repeated the name several times, allowing it to roll off his tongue. He waved the machine gun like a beacon. I prayed its safety catch was still on.

"Phoenix," Althea warned, "I'm not sure about this. We're in a remote area, anything could happen."

"The Tibetan government would not be that stupid. Two accidents aren't going to make much sense. Leaving one of us as a witness would be downright stupid. No one wants to risk an international incident."

"Whatever." She sounded dubious.

We picked our way across the rocky terrain and headed toward the first low building. Four armed officers were crouched in a circle devouring their breakfast or maybe it was a midmorning snack.

I held my pass out to them. All four seemed more interested in us than in any credentials we held. They gave us the once-over. Maybe it was the first time they'd seen two Westernized black women.

The building they guarded looked as if it held records. Inside, a bored-looking clerk manned a reference desk. She leafed through what looked to be a voluminous manual.

"I'd be curious to see what types of books are cataloged there," Althea said. "Some I guarantee are priceless."

"I'm only interested in one statue. I need to get to work."

The building nearby had a disproportionate number of police officers out front. They all toted machine guns and held unlit cigarettes between thumb and forefinger.

"My guess is the statue is in that building," Althea said, and walked quickly in that direction.

"There's going to be a problem getting in," I warned.

"We've come this far. It's worth a try."

We were almost at the building when I spotted a familiar figure at the doorway. I elbowed Althea.

"Please tell me my eyes aren't playing tricks on me."

"They're not."

Cool as the proverbial cucumber, Damon greeted us. "Phe, it's about time you got here. It's taken you long enough."

I kept my voice light. "I thought we were supposed to meet in front of the Main Assembly Hall? Wasn't that the plan?"

He glanced at his watch then back at me. "Plans change. That was half an hour ago."

I didn't realize it was quite that late. "How did you know I'd be here?" I asked.

"Ah, Phe. I know how your mind works."

Amazing. Even I didn't know how my mind worked.

He jutted a thumb in the direction of the interior. "There's not much going on in there. Maitreya's just lying in the closed crate."

I was dying to ask a dozen questions. Instead I said, "You, however, have managed to get in to see her."

Cocky as ever, Damon flashed me his signature smile. "I have my ways. By the way there's a grand unveiling or rather uncrating tomorrow."

"How did you find out?"

"I've been invited. Actually we've been invited. I had Xiong Jing inform the minister that our names needed to be on the invitation list."

It figured. I began to walk into the building. Althea, who'd been taking it all in, fell in step beside me.

"You're wasting your time," Damon said and strolled off. "There really isn't much to see."

I ignored him. Making sure Althea had her credentials in hand, we both entered.

Two guards of East Indian descent pushed off from the wall they were leaning on.

"Madame," one of them said in a deep baritone. "You must have clearance to enter."

I flashed my ID and pass. Then remembering the letter I still carried with its official seal, the one confirming I'd been awarded the assignment, I dug into my tote and handed it over.

The two guards conferred between themselves. The taller of the two held the letter, glancing at me occasionally, then went back to reading. After a while he returned the letter to me and stood aside.

"You may enter."

Althea and I walked in together. As if we'd planned it, we wrapped our arms around our shoulders. Brr. It was at least thirty degrees cooler than outdoors. The hooded wool fleece sweatshirt I wore was no match for this frigid temperature.

A half-dozen men stood or crouched around a small crate. Some were reading a newspaper while others played checkers or chess.

"May I help you?" a Chinese man asked, his accent very British.

I showed him my credentials. "I'm Phoenix Sutherland, retained to restore the idol."

"A man was just here. He already claimed that honor."

"Was that Damon Hernandez by chance?"

"Maybe, maybe not. Tall, dark, muscular?" I nodded. "He was just here a few minutes ago. You have just missed him."

"I'm the person leading this team," I said, puffing out my chest. "Is there a function scheduled for tomorrow? An uncrating of the statue?"

"The official opening of the crate is tomorrow. The contents have already been verified and authenticated. This ceremony means work is soon to begin."

I changed tactics. "Where can I find the gardener who found the statue?"

He shrugged. "There are at least two dozen gardeners that work here. You could ask around."

I realized that was pretty much all I was getting out of him. The folks standing around staring at me were jabbering away in Chinese and Tibetan. Since I didn't speak the languages I didn't have a clue as to what they were saying.

"Let's go," Althea said, heading out.

I followed her.

There was no sign of Damon outside and I presumed he had left. But the sun overhead was warming and felt positively tropical compared to the frigid environment we had just left.

"What now?" Althea asked.

"Let's walk around for a bit. Maybe we'll bump into the gardener."

We wandered around, running into an assortment of workmen cleaning or repairing buildings, but no one looking remotely like a gardener. A choking sound got my attention. I spun around. Tashi was back, waving his pad at me.

"Are you looking for something? Someone?"

I scribbled, "Yes, a gardener. The gardener that found the statue buried in the ground."

Tashi took the notebook back and wrote, "The gardens are over there." He pointed to the left. "I will accompany you if you would like."

I was grateful to have his company. It would save me the time of glancing at a map and figuring out what path to take. Like a little boy, he skipped ahead of us, his robes swishing behind him. He was an odd little man but a happy one. There was something about him I found endearing.

Althea and I huffed and puffed our way up several inclines until we came to a clearing at the top. There several men labored in an Oriental garden complete with pagoda. The men working the ground for the most part appeared to be Tibetan. Their darkened skin and ruddy cheeks gave away their heritage, as did the traditional gear they wore: rough wool pants and a utilitarian vest.

A few of them looked up wearily as I approached.

Tashi's notepad was out. The man closest, thin with stained yellow teeth, spat, narrowly missing the monk's foot. Instead of getting angry, my patient guide's smile widened. He was used to this treatment. Used to being scorned. I hated it.

I did not tolerate such appalling behavior.

Although I assumed most didn't speak English, I didn't care. I meant to get my point across.

"You need to apologize to him," I demanded. "Now."

It was as if I hadn't spoken. The men continued hacking away at the garden beds they'd been working on and chattering amongst themselves.

"Phoenix," Althea called from behind me. "Don't expend your energy on them. They don't know what you're saying and they probably wouldn't care."

I was mad now, furious actually, and getting increasingly more so as the seconds went by. Another fleck of spit caught the hem of Tashi's robe. His smile faltered and then brightened. It was a valiant attempt to say he didn't care.

The obvious contempt and sheer disregard for another human being made my blood boil. I'd spotted the ringleader, the one initiating the spitting. His insolent expression told me all I needed to know. He was used to getting away with this kind of behavior. Not today, not while I was witnessing this situation. He needed to see what it felt like to be shown little respect.

I approached him. When I was almost on top of him he raised his head. Smirking, he said something in Tibetan that was probably not complimentary and spat. His colleagues began laughing and holding their sides. That set me off. My step punch caught him in the lower abdomen. He doubled over and clutched his gut. I glared at the workmen, who'd now turned somber. I was ready to take on any who thought they were my match.

The gardeners' expressions quickly changed. I'd proven that I wouldn't put up with their guff. Tashi was now grinning from ear to ear. He doubled over laughing. Poor Althea was ashen. She'd always hated conflict of any kind.

I curved a hand at Tashi, beckoning him to come forward, and took the pad right out of his hand. I wrote in English, 'Which of you found Maitreya?" then added another note asking Tashi to translate my words into Tibetan.

After he'd done so I held the pad up to the now-silent men and waited for them to read it. One of them started jotting words I did not understand.

"Tashi?" I mouthed, signaling for help. I handed the notepad to him.

The mute monk set about interpreting the man's words.

"He says, 'Yuyi is the one but he did not come in today. His brother is sick and they take him to the hospital.'"

Something niggled at the back of my mind.

Somebody else was sick—Liu Bangfu's, the Minister of Religion and Culture, wife. There must be an influenza going around.

"Tuk too jay," I responded, remembering the words for *thank you* in my phrase book, adding *"Kaba doo menkang?"* Where is the hospital? I'd specifically looked up that phrase.

"I show you," Tashi wrote back.

Althea, who had been taking a great interest in the exchange of the notepad, said to me, "Phoenix, come on, you couldn't be serious. You're just going to show up at a hospital and hope some man you've never met is visiting his brother?"

She had a good point, but I was getting frustrated. Nothing was going as planned. We'd been here almost one week and it had just been hurry up and wait. I needed that bonus and my father's treatments were expensive and growing more pricey by the moment.

"Tomorrow, you take me," I wrote on the notepad.

"You come have tea with me now, *coochee?*"

Coochee meant *please.* I explained the invitation to Althea.

She nodded her head. "At this point, why not. I could use a cup of tea, couldn't you?"

I indicated we would love to and Tashi, very

pleased that we'd accepted his invitation, skipped ahead of us.

We got to his quarters, similar to ours, but instead of cells his was more dormitory style. Definitely not luxurious living accommodations, not when your communal toilet was outdoors.

We were the only ones around when we entered. Despite the bright sunlight outside, the interior was dark and Tashi was forced to light several candles.

He ushered us into what looked to be a dining room. We sat around a battered table, watched him prepare tea and put a handful of biscuits from a tin on a plate. He seemed ecstatic to have company. His was a lonely existence I guessed.

I wondered what role he played in this community of working monks. Tashi's features might be malformed and he was deaf, but otherwise he was sharp as a tack.

I scribbled on the napkin in front of me. "What do you do all day?"

"I am an artist," he scribbled back. "When you are finished with your tea I show you."

I handed his response to Althea. She and I exchanged looks. This was new information. We finished our tea and ate the English biscuits.

Tashi picked up the cups and plates. I motioned to him I would help with the washing up. But he would have none of it. After taking care of the washing he gestured for us to follow him.

With the aid of lit candles, we followed him down several long, dark hallways and up a stairwell which opened into a light airy studio. My breath hitched as I spotted the canvases and the beautiful work.

There were scenes of the Drepung Monastery painted at different times of day. In one crowded corner, unfinished sculptures of a number of deities awaited his touch.

"If he's the artist, he's very talented," Althea whispered, actually looking awed.

"Tashi?" I pointed to the statues, paintings and then at him. I was beginning to catch on that he read lips, as well. "Are those yours?"

Lowering his eyes, he nodded.

"They're beautiful." I approached to get a closer look. I doubted he'd ever received formal training, but even in their primitive raw form they were good. He had a unique way of capturing a scene. I realized this must be a means of self-expression; an outlet by which he got rid of his hurts. My monk friend was full of surprises.

Althea and I oohed, aahed and suitably gushed. Tashi began revealing other pieces he was working on. Then I spotted the painting of the idol.

"Bhaisajyaguru?" I said out loud. "The Medicine Buddha. Also known as the Healing Buddha."

"Yes, said to dispense spiritual medicine when properly worshipped," Althea finished. "He's the one who made twelve vows, one has to do with ethics in healing."

I nodded. "Yes, he is both a spiritual and physical healer."

Tashi pointed to the herb in the Buddha's right hand. He took out his pad and wrote, "If bad person touch. Die."

I'd read something about that. The idol could do both good and bad, depending on who touched it. Must have something to do with one of those vows. If the person was up to no good, a mysterious illness would befall them or a family member, leading to an untimely death.

Something prompted me to write back, "Do you have more paintings of Buddhas?"

Tashi nodded and picked his way to the back of the room, returning with another canvas.

Althea and I openly gawked.

The portrait was an excellent rendition of Maitreya seated upright in its open crate.

"Where did you get this?" I asked, enunciating my words.

He wrote back, "I was there to see the box open."

Chapter 10

The next day it took about fifteen minutes to get to the warehouse where the statue was being uncrated. Judging from the luxury vehicles parked on the side, anyone who was anyone in Tibet had been invited.

Intricate brocading had been draped across the frontage. Butting up against the wall, on either side of the doorway, were two large urns filled with ferns and bright red carnations. Music wafted its way out.

"Looks like the party's on," Damon quipped.

At the entrance, a solemn-looking security person checked our invitations.

At the front of the room, a gold-tasseled rope reserved two-dozen seats for dignitaries. Currently no one was sitting there. People were more intent on mingling and shaking hands.

My focus remained on the raised platform where the crate holding Maitreya was draped in burgundy. There was enough security with machine guns at the ready, to make the boldest of thieves quiver.

Althea tugged on the sleeve of my sweater. "Isn't that Liu Bangfu over there? Maybe we should go over and say hello, and thank him for sending us an invitation."

I looked in the direction she angled her head. Sure enough the esteemed Minister of Religion and Culture was surrounded by a number of important-looking men. The few women accompanying them I guessed to be spouses of the puffed-up dignitaries.

"Over there," Damon hissed. "Look. Madeline Wong's holding court. She has quite the entourage with her."

I glanced over. Indeed, my Chinese friend was swaddled in furs, holding court. The temperature inside certainly didn't warrant it, but the ostentatious outfit was in keeping with her larger-than-life personality. Even from a distance, I saw the monstrous diamonds sparkling in her ears. I needed to go over and thank her. Had it not been for her intervention, Lord only knows where I'd be.

Madeline's group, judging by their clothing, was equally as well-heeled. Most wore designer Western gear. The men in sharp suits and the women in ornate cocktail dresses that shouted Paris couture.

"Shall we make the rounds?" I asked. Without waiting for a response, I began easing my way to the front of the room.

Madeline looked up from an animated conversation and spotted me. She curved a crimson nail in my direction. I headed over.

"Phoenix, how nice you look," she gushed. "You, too, Althea. And, Damon, well, Damon, you are just too handsome. Oh, to be young again." She kissed us on both cheeks, continental style.

"Thanks so much for the invitation," I whispered when she enveloped me in a perfumed embrace.

"We shall talk when this is over with. Yes?"

Madeline began introducing us to the people around her, none of whose names I remembered. I did, however, note the words *historical preservation society,* mentioned a time or two.

"Have you met Phoenix Sutherland?" Madeline said to a gentleman outfitted in traditional Tibetan gear. She introduced the man as the honorable Kalon Nyandek. "Phoenix is the restorer leading the reconstruction team."

The silver-haired man bowed and beamed a white smile my way. "Yes, indeed. She is the artist we hired on your recommendation. It is indeed a pleasure to meet you, Ms. Sutherland."

An official-looking woman had climbed onto the stage. Flanked by guards, she stood in front of the crimson-draped crate. When she held her hands up, the room immediately quieted. Some folks began shuffling into those roped-off seats.

"Sit with us," Madeline mouthed, heading for the gold-tasseled area. We did not need a second invitation. We followed her.

The woman on stage spoke in Tibetan for about ten minutes. She paused only to acknowledge applause. Liu Bangfu, the Minister of Religion and Culture, joined her onstage. He, too, spoke in Tibetan and then switched to English. He acknowledged Damon and the team of women he'd brought along to restore such a valuable antiquity. And he thanked us for taking the long journey here.

I tried to hide my outrage behind a bland expression. When he was through, Madeline whispered in my ear. "The woman, her name is Nina

Chien, she is the president of the historical society and a very good person to know."

A number of people mounted the stage, mostly men. They joined Liu Bangfu. Among them was Kalon Nyandek, the other minister.

The security guards' expressions grew fierce. The music, previously soothing, swelled. With purpose, Nina Chien stepped forward and swept the velvet throw off the crate.

An expectant silence followed. Those who were seated up front craned their necks, not wanting to miss one second of this auspicious occasion. Workmen, who'd been lolling around, peeled themselves off the walls and, bringing tools with them, set to work opening the lid of the crate.

And the music played on. The lid was off and set aside. Liu Bangfu, Kalon Nyandek and a host of others moved forward to inspect the contents.

A strangled gasp came from the Chien woman, followed by a number of barked orders.

I looked to Madeline Wong for an interpretation. But she, like most of the seated people, was on her feet.

On stage all hell had broken loose.

I sprang from my seat and raced onto the platform. Damon was right behind me. The security men were busy trying to hold back out-of-control guests who'd bounded onto the stage. They were outnumbered. Ducking around people, Damon and I pushed our way to a point where we could see the open crate.

A gaping hole lay where Maitreya was supposed to be.

The statue was missing.

Chapter 11

"I needed this," I said, an hour later, hefting my beer mug and clinking it against Damon's and Althea's glasses.

We were at a local bar. The people around us, engaged in conversation, were oblivious to what had happened a short time ago.

Once it was discovered Maitreya was missing, we'd been ordered to evacuate the building. In the crush to get out I'd lost Madeline. I planned on touching base with her later to thank her again for her help and find out what she knew.

With nothing else to do, we'd decided to go in

search of local entertainment. After wandering aimlessly for a while, we'd found this delightful local café with an enchanting view from the rooftop. We'd plopped ourselves down to regroup and unwind. We needed to come up with a plan quickly.

"What if the statue's never found?" Althea said, voicing my unspoken thoughts.

"Then the government will have to make the decision to send us home," I answered. "The good thing is we're being paid to sit and wait."

I didn't necessarily feel that way. There was still my father's situation to consider. Should we be sent home I might never be able to clear his name, and of course there was the matter of his expensive medical care.

"True," Damon added, "but even if Maitreya is found, you'll need to renegotiate a new deadline, Phe. We'll have to work pretty much night and day as it is."

I'd thought about that. We'd been held up from beginning work through no fault of our own.

"I'll request a meeting with Xiong Jing tomorrow and get an update. Liu Bangfu should be there, as well. We'll need word from an official government representative as to the plans to proceed."

"The man's pretty much ignored us all along.

What makes you think he'll even show up?" Damon said sagely.

"Because I intend to find him wherever he is. I'll involve Madeline if need be. She wields a lot of power in this town."

"And we'll owe her our lives." Althea eyed me over the rim of her mug. I could tell she was getting pretty fed up with all of this.

"What do we do, meanwhile? More exploring, sightseeing, book reading, jogging?" Damon's expression was droll.

"We'll stay busy," I said, injecting optimism I didn't have into my voice.

And as long as you stay the hell away from me, I'll be okay. I want no repeat of the other night.

"I know what I'm going to do," Althea piped up. "I'm going to do what I keep saying I should. I'll take this opportunity to read up on the three statues. It's fascinating that three clay statues made by a humble artesian monk could become so valuable. I'm curious about the artist and I need to find out more about Manjushri, the Buddha of wisdom. He's the one I know the least about."

"Good plan." Although he said the words, Damon seemed contemplative. He sipped his beer and turned his full attention on me. For a moment I was lost in his gray gaze.

"What will you be doing, Phe?" he asked.

"Exploring. Becoming more familiar with the monastery's grounds."

"I wouldn't wander too far if I were you."

Was that a veiled threat?

"I'm capable of taking care of myself," I shot back.

Damon took a swig of his beer. "Just in case, I'll be shadowing you. Don't leave without telling either me or Althea where you're going."

"You will not."

"I will, too."

Althea cleared her throat. "Uhh. Children!"

It was déjà vu for her all over again. She'd sat through a million of our spats.

I needed to get out of there and put space between me and Damon. I stood, threw a handful of yuan on the table and headed out.

"Chill, Phe," Damon called after me.

I didn't bother answering.

"Then wait up."

Ignoring him, I raced from the restaurant.

I needed this time alone. I'd thought I was completely over Damon but now I wasn't sure. My fault for sleeping with him, I supposed.

Out on the streets, the air was crisp and invigorating. I wandered the alleys, at times glancing over my shoulder, hoping that Damon had not carried through on his threat and followed me.

A tug on my jacket stopped me midstep. I swung around prepared to blast Damon.

"Tashi!" I said. "It's nice to see you."

He thrust his notepad at me. "What is this? Our future Buddha has disappeared?"

I scribbled back. "How did you find out?"

"Word travels quickly. Maybe we need to find the gardener that found the statue?"

I scribbled back. "Sure."

I wondered if I was being set up. I still hadn't figured out what Tashi had to gain by befriending me. I looked into his unsightly face but saw no guile. We headed back in the direction I'd come from.

I stopped for a second to scribble, "How do you know the gardener's working today?"

Tashi scribbled back. "I am taking you to his home."

Noting my puzzled expression, he quickly filled me in. "His brother has taken a turn for the worse. They think he may die."

"Then this is not a good time. I should not intrude."

"This is a very good time."

Cryptic, but now my curiosity was piqued. We continued through winding streets, the altitude making me huff and puff. Finally we came to a simple home in dire need of repair.

"We are here," Tashi wrote.

"Now we do what?" I asked.

"We find your gardener and see if he will talk."

The sounds of chanting came from inside the house. Two men walked by us, carrying what looked like white material draped over their arms.

"They are preparing for death," Tashi scribbled.

"You go into the house. I will wait here," I wrote.

Tashi nodded and ducked into the open door while I waited for what seemed an eternity outside. Finally he emerged, bringing with him a shrunken man who seemed barely five feet tall. He nodded at me and appeared preoccupied with his own thoughts.

There would be problems communicating. How to explain what I needed to know?

Tashi passed me his notepad.

"I told him you are Phoenix and in my country to repair the Buddha he found."

"What is his name? And can you ask him where exactly the statue was found?" I wrote back.

Tashi scribbled and handed the pad over to the anguished little man.

"He says his name is Yuyi. He dug up the crate when he was digging in the gardens of the monastery. He said he already told this to his boss."

"Where exactly in the gardens?" I wrote back and waited for Tashi to translate.

My question produced a shrug. Taking the notepad back, I tried another approach.

"Ask him what's wrong with his brother."

Yuyi shrugged and made a fanning motion, then pointed to his tongue.

Tashi translated this to mean having a swollen tongue and a fever.

"He says he must now go back inside."

"Just one more question. Who is his boss?"

But the gardener had already retreated into his house.

I stood totally still for a minute trying to get my bearings and figure out what next. I could return to the convent or go back to the restaurant and see if Althea and Damon were still there. But first I needed to make a phone call.

I crossed the road again, found Tashi and scribbled on his pad that I needed to find a phone. He bowed and gestured for me to follow him.

We wove our way back through streets filled with backpackers, pilgrims and monks young enough to need parental supervision. Meanwhile, I kept my eyes peeled.

Tashi slowed in front of a long, low building. A sign in English announced it to be an Internet Café.

"I need a telephone," I scribbled, thinking perhaps he'd misunderstood.

"Inside."

Not expecting him to wait, I thanked him and entered the drafty building. It was a busy place inside. Tourists of varying nationalities sat in front of computers e-mailing relatives and friends, while a line of students and tourists patiently waited their turn.

I considered sending a quick message to Aunt Esther to check up on my father. The last time we'd talked he'd been taking a new experimental medication. But I couldn't afford to stand in a long line.

A bored clerk sat in a booth eyeing the customers. I handed over the requisite yuan, and in return got a slip of paper with a number written on it. I was pointed to a waiting area.

Ten minutes went by before I was called to a phone. By now I had Madeline's number memorized and quickly dialed the rotary phone. I was surprised and overjoyed when she answered.

"It's Phoenix," I said, when she'd completed her greeting. "I'm glad you made it home safe and sound."

"Hello, darling, it's good to hear from you, too."

"I have a favor to ask," I said.

"Anything for you, my darling."

Madeline sounded amazingly upbeat.

"Can you implore Liu Bangfu to show up at just one of our meetings? We've been dealing with Xiong Jing and frankly not getting anywhere. Now that Maitreya has disappeared we need to know what to expect. Every deadline that has been established will need to be changed."

"I'll see what I can do."

"What's the latest?" I asked. "Is there any speculation as to what might have happened to Maitreya?"

"Lots of speculation. Some say it's the Taliban. You may have recalled how they destroyed the Buddhas of Bamiyan a few years back?"

I did and it was a heinous act.

"The other thought," Madeline said, "is that the statue might have been stolen by a religious zealot, someone wanting to bring it to the Dalai Lama in exile as a gift."

Food for thought.

"And there is another consideration. A Chinese militia group might have stolen it. They may have wanted to drive home the point they are in charge."

"Certainly something to think about," I said.

The agent outside held up a card. Two Minutes Left.

"You must go. I'll do my best to bring a meeting about. Word about the statue's disappearance has already spread and the government has their hands full. Come tomorrow, every Buddhist in this country will be demanding action or sitting in silent protest."

We were disconnected. I hung up the phone feeling no more optimistic than when I'd started out.

Tashi wasn't anywhere to be seen when I left the building. Glancing at my watch, I realized that between waiting and making my call at least a half an hour had passed. Soon curfew would be enforced.

I paid my few yuan and hopped into a minivan which would take me back to the monastery.

By the time I was dropped off I was fighting mad.

Mad enough to do something about it.

Chapter 12

I slept fitfully that night. Worn-out, and bleary-eyed, I awoke early and decided to go for a run.

There was a distinct chill in the air and it took me some time to warm up. I did a series of stretches and bends as quickly as I could then I began jogging slowly, following the pilgrims' route west of the perimeter wall and heading in the direction of Gephel Ritro. I would never make it all the way uphill, besides there was the time to consider. Twenty minutes later, I doubled back and headed toward the area Tashi had taken me where the rude gardener was working.

I jogged in one place while looking out on beautifully tended gardens. I hoped to catch a glimpse of Yuyi. A crazy idea, I knew. Conversation would be difficult without a translator. But what other options did I really have? Who would have the answers to what I needed to know?

"Good morning."

The voice was singsongy, but definitely male. He spoke English, heavily accented English, but English no less.

"Good morning," I responded automatically.

"Looks like it's going to be a beautiful day."

"Let's hope so."

A tall, gray-haired man, dark in complexion, stood next to me doing a series of stretches and bends. Judging by his heavily accented English, I thought he might be East Indian or Pakistani.

"My name is Niall Brahma," he said after a while. "I own an art gallery and antiquities store in town. You are the artist here to restore our missing Maitreya?"

"I'm Phoenix Sutherland."

I found it both interesting and disconcerting that he knew who I was.

"I always thought it very strange," he said in conversational tones, "that this statue, which has been missing for years, has all of a sudden been found on the grounds of this property."

He was echoing my thoughts exactly. There were times it was wise to listen and not comment. This was one of them.

"I find it even odder that considering what its discovery means to the Buddhist world, the statue would not have been more tightly secured day and night. There's been hoopla and press, and you were brought here all the way from America to restore the idol. Now, poof—" he made a clicking sound with his fingers "—it is gone."

"What are you saying?" I waited for him to go on.

"I am saying it has to be an inside job or someone trying to make a political statement. Maitreya is, after all, a statue of some significance. He is the Universal Christ. Buddhists today await his coming in the same manner that Christians await Jesus's second coming."

Ears wide-open now, I nodded. I could tell he liked to pontificate.

"Come midmorning you should see some activity on the streets. The Buddhists will be up in arms and there will be many peaceful protests."

"I would think the PSB would break them up."

"Oh, they will try. Some may even be arrested."

Niall seemed a chatty fellow. I wondered why he had chosen me of all people to strike up a conversation with?

"You're rather well-informed," I said carefully.

"I have to be. I've lived in Lhasa over twenty years. I came here on a visit and ended up marrying a local woman. Despite a great deal of opposition, I set up a business. When you deal in art and antiquities, you know everything there is to know in the art world. You keep an ear to the ground."

A thought occurred to me, one I immediately voiced. "You must speak Tibetan well then?"

"Yes, along with Hindi, English, as you can tell, and a smattering of Chinese."

There was a reason he'd found me.

"If it's not too much of an imposition, would you mind if we continued our conversation as we walked through the gardens?"

"Not at all."

"I have so many questions and you seem so knowledgeable."

"Any particular reason our stroll needs to take place through the gardens? There are some lovely walkways."

Smart man.

Since I had nothing to lose, I opted for honesty.

"I was fortunate enough to be introduced to the gardener who found the statue yesterday. I wanted to ask him some more questions."

"And you need my Tibetan," Niall finished.

"Yes, I need your Tibetan."

"Then I am at your service." Niall offered his arm.

Although I wasn't entirely sure of him, I took the arm he offered and followed him down a winding path. We strolled for a while with no one paying us the least bit of attention. I scanned the horizon, remembering that Yuyi was very short.

Niall slowed down in front of a group of men working on a rock garden. He called to them in rapid Tibetan. Finally, one of the men responded and pointed a finger in the distance.

Niall turned back to me. "Your Yuyi is here. He is working the grounds in front of the Tshomchen. Shall we head there?"

He didn't wait for an answer. He began walking in that direction and taking me with him. He seemed very familiar with the grounds of the monastery but I suppose that was to be expected given that he had lived in Lhasa these past twenty years.

"You think maybe we've been sent on a wild-goose chase?" I asked.

"Let's just wait a while and see if our gardener shows up."

A few early-morning walkers and joggers went by. A handful of tourists up early, stopped to snap photos.

"There's your man," Niall said when I had all but given up.

And there he was with a wheelbarrow in hand, carting what looked to be topsoil. Almost forgetting I needed Niall to interpret, I sped off in Yuyi's direction. Niall followed on my heels.

Yuyi set his wheelbarrow down and looked as if he was about to run. The poor man was probably wondering why this crazy black woman was stalking him.

Niall's soothing tones seemed to calm him down but he kept a wary eye on me.

"Yuyi said you came to his home yesterday," Niall said, looking at me curiously.

"I did."

"He said you were with the ugly monk."

"I was with Tashi," I admitted, inwardly bristling. My kindly monk's looks had grown on me.

"He wonders what you want with him."

"I just want him to answer some questions. I want to know exactly where he found the crate holding Maitreya and if he opened it."

Niall translated my questions. I waited while the gardener let loose with a flow of words.

"He said you asked him that very same question yesterday, and he answered it as best as he could."

"Tell him to show you exactly where he found the statue."

After Niall was done, I noticed Yuyi's body stiffen. He pointed a vague finger in the other direction. We weren't getting anywhere. I changed tactics.

"Ask him what he did when he found the statue. Let me rephrase that. Ask him who was the first person he showed the statue to."

I waited for his reply.

"His brother."

"The sick one?"

"Yes."

"Then what did they do?"

"Went to find his boss, he says, and turned it over."

"Who is his boss?" I shot back.

"That depends on which day it is."

We were going around in circles.

I made a bold move. "Tell Yuyi he'd better come up with a name quickly, because if he doesn't, I'm going to complain to the people at the front gate and tell them he was rude to me. He'll lose his job. He won't have money for his brother's medicine."

"You are tough," Niall said, smiling at me. "But it may very well work."

He repeated my words or at least that's what I thought. The little man looked petrified. He began speaking quickly and in a pitch that indicated his anxiety. I stuck my hand in the pocket of my cargo pants, retrieved a handful of yuan and handed it to Niall to give to him.

"Tell him that I'm staying here on the premises, over at the convent. If he remembers anything else, anything at all, there's more where that came from."

The offer brought forth the first smile from the previously uncooperative gardener. Wheelbarrow in hand he trotted off.

By then the sun had emerged and more and more people were strolling through the grounds. I thanked Niall for his help and told him I needed to head back.

He pressed a card into my hand. "Come for tea soon. I will show you my little art gallery and you can meet my wife. She will enjoy the company of an American woman."

"Thank you. I'd like that."

I placed his card in the pocket of my running shorts, shook his hand and headed off in the other direction.

The day had just begun. Anything could happen.

Chapter 13

"Hey, Phe. I've been looking all over for you," Damon greeted me, the minute I walked into the convent. He was freshly showered and dressed in tailored jeans and a formfitting polo shirt. The shirt clung to his muscular arms and emphasized his broad chest and taut torso. He eyed me up and down.

"We're needed at Minister Bangfu's temporary offices. An emergency meeting's been called. I have the address written down." He patted his shirt pocket.

I smelled Madeline Wong behind this.

"How much time do I have?"

Damon glanced at his TAG Heuer. "About fifteen minutes. There's a car coming to pick us up."

I dashed off, making a beeline for the communal showers. Lucky for me the process of showering and dressing was not a complicated one. I threw on a pair of jeans, tugged on a turtleneck, swept my hair up into a pony and was done in fifteen minutes.

Ten minutes later, our hired vehicle pulled up in front of the Minister of Religion and Culture's new offices.

Damon flanked me as I entered the modern glass and brick structure. I'd expected to find Xiong Jing waiting in the lobby, but there was no sign of him.

"What floor?" I asked Damon.

"Sixth."

"Any thoughts as to what we're about to hear?" Damon asked quietly.

I shrugged. "Either we're about to be released and sent home, or it's more sit around and wait."

"I've had just about as much sitting around as I can take."

In my head I calculated what the government owed us in terms of expenses. It would be spit in a bucket compared to what I'd expected to make, plus there would be no bonus.

Contingency plan number two would have to be put into action, much as I hated it. If we were about to be sent home I would have to get a second mortgage on the studio. That way I would at least have enough money to ensure my father got the help he needed.

I had promised myself never to put myself in that much debt. But desperate times called for desperate measures. I would do just about anything for my dad. He'd been the one who'd supported my choices. He'd always been there for me.

Damon squeezed my hand. "You okay, Phe?"

"I'm fine." I squared my shoulders.

Holding on to Damon's hand like an anchor, I strolled through smoked glass doors.

"Good morning," Damon announced. "Minister Bangfu is expecting us."

She looked up. A flicker of surprise registered before her expression became neutral.

"Good morning. Yes, the minister is expecting you. Please take a seat." She waved us into two upholstered chairs in a cozy nook.

"Would you like tea?" she asked.

I wondered what had brought on this new wave of politeness. I also wondered if these were more stalling tactics.

"We'd both like a cup of tea," Damon said, speaking for me. I shot him a look.

In a few minutes the secretary returned bearing a tray with a teapot and cups. I moved aside the magazines so she could set down the tray.

"How long will we be waiting?" I asked pointedly.

"Oh, not long. Your project manager should be here any minute." She glanced at a watch circling her tiny wrist.

"I'm glad to see you survived," I said equally as polite, and perhaps a tinge sarcastic. "The last time you and I met the government building had to be evacuated."

She shot me a watery smile. "It is good to be alive."

Another twenty minutes went by. Even Mr. Calm, Cool and Collected was getting irritated. I could tell by the rapid tapping of his boot tips. Another ten minutes.

Enough was enough. I set my third cup of tea down, clinking the saucer loudly and got up.

Forgoing any pretense of politeness I approached the secretary and asked, "How much longer?"

She seemed flustered. "I don't know. Mr. Xiong Jing should have shown up by now."

"Can you call him?"

She hesitated.

"You must have his number or at the very

least your boss has it." Damon's voice came from behind me.

The woman looked up at us, debated for a second and then made up her mind. She picked up the receiver and punched in some numbers.

"Sir," she squeaked, "the Americans are still waiting. Mr. Xiong Jing is not here and they are…well, getting restless… oh, all right, sir, I will tell them."

I waited for her to set down the receiver and stood arms akimbo. "Well?"

"Mr. Bangfu wants you to wait just a moment longer. He will try to make some calls."

Damon and I exchanged charged glances.

"What does a moment longer mean?" he asked.

"You must be patient."

She was pushing her luck. Couple that with resenting her patronizing manner, and disliking her boss, I was this close to exploding.

"Breathe, Phe," Damon said under his breath.

The secretary's phone rang. She broke her gaze to answer.

A sob tore from her throat. "I am so sorry. So sorry. I will let the minister know. He will call you, all right."

She was up and halfway across the room before I caught her.

I blocked her path. "What's going on?"

Her stoic expression broke. Her eyes swam with tears.

"Mr. Xiong Jing has been killed," she said quietly. "That was his brother-in-law who called. He died in a car accident on his way here."

My jaw flapped open. Damon's arms wrapped around me, keeping me steady. I leaned into him, drawing strength from his warmth. I was glad for his solid presence. He held me close to his chest while I took long, deep, calming breaths.

"Let's go. Phe," he said, edging me toward the door. "There's nothing more to be accomplished here." To the secretary he said, "Have someone, preferably your minister, get in touch with us later."

Over her shoulder, the secretary gave us the same sad-eyed look. "I shall tell the minister to call."

When we returned to the convent, we met up with Althea. She regarded us through narrowed golden eyes. "Something's up."

Damon filled her in.

"Oh, no. Phoenix, I'm really scared," she admitted. "I think maybe we should go home."

I shook my head. "We've gotten this far and we need to see this thing through."

Chapter 14

I woke up in the middle of the night wondering if I'd had a bad dream. A scraping, rattling noise penetrated my sleep. Glancing at the illuminated face of the clock, I realized it was closer to early morning than the dead of the night as I'd thought.

Now wide-awake, I heard the noise again. A handful of gravel set my windowpane rattling. I flew from my bed and pressed my nose against the glass of the cell's solitary window. Black was slowly giving away to gray and I thought I saw a shadow move quickly across the grounds.

Dressed in a long T-shirt that skimmed my

knees, and knee socks because it was cold, I crept from my room and down the long hallway.

At the entrance, I eased open the door and stepped out. I stubbed my toe against something and pitched forward.

"Son of a…"

A foreign object obstructed my path. I wobbled then steadied myself. I reached out to feel what was in my way. It felt like a box.

My caution buttons went on high. My palms were already clammy. A wave of queasiness almost brought me to my knees at the thought of what might be in that box. My imagination ricocheted out of control. What if it was a slaughtered goat? Even worse, what if it was a dead body?

I braced myself, thinking that maybe what I needed to do was find a flashlight. But that would mean leaving the box unattended and who knew if it would be there on my return.

I wrapped my arms around the object, assessing it and confirming that it was a cardboard box. I considered lifting it up but my imagination had gone haywire again. It could be a bomb. As I stood for a moment considering the best course of action to take, a wide sweeping light illuminated my face.

"Phe?"

No one else in the world ever called me Phe. "Damon?"

He'd obviously been out walking or something. The flashlight he used to light his way now focused on my face, and swept my body. It also prevented me from seeing him. I guessed that he wore dark clothes.

"What are you doing up?" he asked.

"I could ask you the same."

"I had trouble sleeping."

"Something or someone woke me up. Obviously they wanted me here."

The flashlight arced, creating a wider beam.

"What's that?" Damon asked as the light played across the carton.

"I don't know," I answered honestly. "It just appeared."

It was slowly dawning on me just how cold I was. I could feel my nipples stiffen and brush the thin material of the T-shirt. The last thing I'd expected was to run into anyone, and most certainly not Damon.

He came closer. I was right. He was wearing black jeans, a black leather bomber jacket and a matching formfitting T-shirt. He even had on a black knitted cap, the type that you pulled on and cuffed. He shrugged out of his jacket and handed it to me.

"You're freezing, Phe."

The rays from his flashlight swept the box again.

"Might as well see what's in there," he added, getting down on one knee.

"No, don't." I didn't want him touching that box. I reached over and grabbed his shoulders. "It might be a bomb."

"Relax, babe." He placed an ear to the box. Then looked back at me. "There's nothing ticking in there. Didn't you say someone woke you up? If they wanted to kill you they would have done it while you slept. They didn't have a problem setting a building afire and bombing government property so why would they think twice?"

Good point. Even so, he nudged the box with a tip of his boot. My heart in my hand, I made sure to stand clear. Getting braver, Damon kicked out at the box. It didn't skitter, didn't even move.

The first rays of dawn now streaked the sky.

"Okay, I'm opening it up," Damon announced, handing me his flashlight. He removed a penknife from his pocket and slit the tape holding the flaps together. "Ready?"

I was not. I prepared myself for the worse. I expected to find some dismembered animal or bloody human part.

"Come closer," Damon urged. "Shine the flashlight inside."

I aimed the light at the opening, but kept my head turned. I just wasn't up to dealing with gore.

Damon whooshed out a breath. "Look what we have here."

I moved closer.

"Phe. Keep that light trained right there." Reaching down into the box, Damon removed a medium-size clay statue. "Behold," he said, sounding completely awed as he held the idol up to the light, "our missing Maitreya."

I gasped and gazed at the idol with its greenish-blue hue. He was a glorious piece of work even though his crown was chipped and his jewelry had seen better days. The throne on which he sat in the full cross-legged position needed repair. A stump was in the place where his right hand should have been. It would have touched his cheek had a hand been there.

Overall he was in poor shape but I knew good work when I saw it. And this was big and good. Someone had lovingly created this image and paid enormous attention to detail.

Maitreya was the reason I was here. I had been granted the honor of restoring him. And when I restored him, I'd be restoring my father.

"We'll need to get him inside right away," Damon insisted. "Before whoever brought him to us changes their minds. Someone might very well have followed the person." He thrust the statue into my arms. "Forget the box. Cover him with my coat."

We headed for Damon's cell. I set the statue on the floor and locked the door. Damon brought over a straight-back chair to place under the knob. The sun was rising by then and there was enough light coming through the one window to see Maitreya in all his glory.

I handed him to Damon, who set him down in front of an altar draped in a pristine white cloth. On it was incense, a miniature Buddha and a plate of fruit; an offering I assumed. I stood there for a moment watching Damon, who'd closed his eyes. He had his head bowed, paying homage to his messiah, the long-awaited teacher.

When Damon finally opened his eyes, he smiled at me. He seemed at peace. "I don't know about you, but I'm dying to get to work on this piece," he said.

"We'll need to contact someone about our discovery," I said. "Any thoughts? There'll be a million questions asked. No one will believe the statue was just left on our front door."

"Agreed. But for the next hour or two I plan to just enjoy him. If he turns out to be the real deal, it will mean everything to the Buddhist world. Our long-awaited teacher will soon return and we will achieve another stage of enlightenment."

I digested what he had said and tried to translate it into Baptist terms. It would be like the second coming of Christ.

I thought it might be wise to go back to my room before everyone awakened, but thought better of it. I didn't plan on leaving Damon alone with that statue. I didn't exactly trust him, and it seemed strange he would be out and about at that hour of the morning taking a walk.

It was too early to call Madeline. And the only other person that might know more about the statue than he was letting on was the gallery owner, Niall Brahma. And him I didn't exactly trust, either.

"Damon, don't you think you and I should make a concerted effort to authenticate the idol before turning it in? It might mean working night and day, but at least we'll know something."

Damon's light-colored eyes lit up. He swung me off my feet. "Capital idea, Phe."

When he let me down, I stuck out my hand.

"Deal then."

Instead of shaking hands, he kissed me on the mouth and said softly, "Deal!" Our kiss was meant to be in lieu of a handshake but somehow it segued into a melding of tongues; a passionate acceptance that despite our trials, tribulations, ups and downs, the desire for each other was still very real.

I stepped out of Damon's embrace before things got out of hand. Memories of our passionate night flooded my mind.

But now we had something to accomplish and we had limited time to do it.

"What about Althea? Are we getting her involved?" Damon asked.

I shook my head. I loved my girlfriend, but the fewer people who knew about our finding Maitreya, the better. Besides, this was all about authentication not reconstruction.

We'd been told earlier the statue's authenticity had been verified and that our job would be one of restoration and reconstruction. But we needed to see for ourselves. No point in wasting the grant monies the government had been awarded if this wasn't really Maitreya, or at least the Maitreya we were expecting to find, the one created back in 500 B.C.

"When would you like to start?" I asked.

"In a couple of hours. I'm suddenly tired now. I need some shut-eye."

Was that a subtle way of telling me I needed to go to my room?

I yawned. "I'll join you," I said, looking pointedly at the bed. But just the thought of lying next to Damon scared me. It would be hell; I would want to touch him again and in the most intimate of places.

"Sure you want to do that?" he asked, yanking off the formfitting T-shirt to reveal a broad bronze chest with a silky patch of hair that covered his pectorals and trailed downward under his waistband. "We're not going to get much sleep."

I couldn't help staring. He was in magnificent shape for thirty-four. He slipped off his boots and slid out of his pants. The briefs he wore were a silky black and clung to his sculptured buttocks. His solid thighs and muscular calves bespoke the athlete he once was. He'd played football through high school and college in a rough area where no one played by the rules.

But Damon had turned down an athletic scholarship to college knowing that his heart wasn't in sports. He'd loved art and antiques and he'd loved science and so he'd gone with his heart.

Damon stuck a thumb under the waistband of his underpants.

I cleared my throat. "Uh, maybe you should wait."

"Why, Phe?" He left them on, thank God and slid under the covers, curling a finger at me. "*Venga aqui,* babe. Let me keep you warm."

I was beginning to regret my decision to keep watch on Maitreya, but determined to follow through. I joined him in bed but ensured a comfortable space remained between us. Even so I sensed, no, felt the heat radiating from his skin and resisted the urge to luxuriate in it.

Damon wrapped a sinewy arm around me and inhaled. "I love the way you smell."

I wanted to shrug out from under that arm, but the truth was, having Damon hold me made me feel protected. Blessed. There was something almost mystical about being in a chilly cell with an altar in the corner, a supposedly rare and precious Buddha in our possession that was both intimate and special.

I lay there on my side, eyes closed, pretending to sleep, ignoring the fact that Damon's hands had slipped under my T-shirt and were now massaging my back and buttocks. And that he had wedged himself up against me until I could feel the swelling of his erection.

His hands were around my waist now, his fingers drawing patterns on my stomach. Those same hands crept upward to claim my breasts, kneading and rubbing until the nipples stiffened and hardened. I was rubbing then bucking against him. My thighs opened of their own accord. Damon freed himself, paused to look for protection on the nightstand, and then sheathed, slid my panties aside.

He slid a finger in me, checking to make sure I was moist and ready for him. He entered me using long confident strokes. My muscles contracted, released and contracted again. Soon we fell into an easy, comfortable rhythm.

I bit down on his shoulder. He grabbed my butt, and when he entered me again, I went with it, soaring, experiencing both the pleasure and frenzy that came with good loving.

Chapter 15

Two hours later I woke up wrapped in Damon's arms. I didn't want to think about what had happened or how easy it had been to fall back into an old pattern. I slid out from under him, made sure his door was unlocked and headed for my room. The Maitreya could wait for a few minutes. It would have to. I hoped to God I didn't run into Althea. I quickly got dressed.

When I returned he was stirring restlessly and mumbling something in his sleep.

"Damon," I whispered.

He did it again. I realized he was calling out my name.

"Phe." Snore. "Phe."

I sat on the side of the bed and pushed on his bare shoulder. Damon's skin was flushed with sleep and he felt warm underhand. The sheets lay lightly draped over one hip. I stared down at his magnificent body, awed by the hard muscles that bunched. In repose he looked every inch the athlete that he once was. I resisted the urge to climb back into bed and snuggle next to him.

"Damon," I called, shaking him roughly. "Wake up. We have business to take care of."

"Uugh." Snore.

"Damon!"

One eye popped open and then the other.

"What, Phe? Are you cold?"

"We've got to get to work on Maitreya."

That got him sitting up. His curly hair was sticking out in all the wrong places and he reminded me of a little boy.

"You're dressed, no fair," he said.

I cut my eyes at him. "You need to be dressed, too."

Damon climbed out of bed and I turned away, not wanting to think about how physically close we'd been just a few hours ago. He strode across the room buck naked, still groggy and looking for a bathroom.

"It's down the hallway, remember, but you'll need to get dressed," I reminded him.

After he'd left, I found myself standing in front of the altar again, fascinated by this serene place of worship. I thought perhaps that by allowing my brain to go numb I would gain some of Damon's centeredness.

Picking up the statue, I examined its severed limb. It could either have been damaged or deliberately lopped off. The color, though, was what had always bothered me. Maitreya was supposed to be yellow and not greenish-blue.

I had a sudden brainstorm. If someone had wanted to disguise a statue they would get rid of the major identifiers. If the hand had held something in it like the stem of a plant then it would have to be removed. And if the statue had a distinctive color, then one would need to paint over it. Blue and yellow paint mixed would produce a bluish-green hue.

What was taking Damon so long, I wondered? I wanted to run this crazy, or maybe not so crazy, idea by him. There were the mysterious illnesses that the gardener's brother and Liu Bangfu's wife were afflicted with, and there was the unexpected death of our project manager.

Then the thought occurred to me. What if I were holding Bhaisajyaguru, the Medicine Buddha, in my hand and not Maitreya? It might sound preposterous but it should be considered.

Damon was back.

"What are you cooking up in that brain of yours?" he asked as I stood there pensive.

I voiced my suspicions, which didn't seem at all to surprise him. "Well, I guess the faster we get to work, the faster we'll find out if your theory is right." He rustled through his gear and got his camera out.

"I'm going to record areas of discontinuity," he said, in scientist mode now. "I'll look for apparent alterations, et cetera, then later I'll examine them with infrared and ultraviolet techniques. Since we aren't going to be able to keep the statue forever, I'll do the best that I can. We'll need to get the missing idol back before we're accused of theft and carted off to jail."

Not a pleasant thought, and certainly not one I hadn't thought of.

"What do you have there?" I asked as Damon brought over additional gear.

"My tungsten lamps. I'll arrange them at very shallow angles to the surface. In this business it's known as raked lighting. It's a good way to pick up surface defects and other abnormalities and alterations."

I stood by and watched him take his photographs.

"How will they be developed?" I asked.

"I'll think of something."

I'd come to a decision. "I'll try reaching Madeline Wong. She'll know what to do about Maitreya."

"I wish we weren't so dependent on her. She's been a good friend but can you trust her?"

"Probably about as much as I can trust you."

"Ouch, that hurt! I'll go with you to the Telecom building so that you can make that phone call. It's probably not advisable to discuss anything sensitive on these premises, even if we could find a phone. We'll take Maitreya with us."

I watched him carefully wrap the eighteen-inch statue into two towels and stuff it into his backpack. For a fleeting moment I wondered if it was Damon who didn't trust me, and that his insistence on accompanying me was to hear what I would say to Madeline.

"You can if you'd like," I agreed. "But on the way back we need to stop off and get something to eat. I'm starving."

In the back of the taxi, Damon caught me up on his life. The backpack holding Maitreya was on the floor between his ankles. He'd gone back to New York after we broke up. He'd worked for several private clients while I'd stayed on in Florence, completing the restoration job that had created the rift between us.

Damon then jumped on the opportunity to free-lance for a museum in Buenos Aires. He'd stayed there for a while working on a number of projects. Reading between the lines, I gathered there'd been a romance that hadn't worked out.

Just like ours hadn't.

After that, it had been Tokyo, Hong Kong and Singapore. For the last three years he'd been in Europe, living in France for part of the time. He'd then been commissioned by the queen of England to work on her private collection. He'd traveled through Italy: Milan, Florence, Rome, where there was no shortage of work, and after Rosa, his mother, died he'd come home to wrap up her affairs.

"What about you, Phe?" he asked. "Did you ever marry?"

I shook my head. "I've had no time for relationships. They take up too much time and energy."

"That's sad. *Que lastima!* What a pity!" He made me sound as if I were a hopeless cause.

"Have you been married?" I countered, ignoring my fluttering stomach. I shouldn't care. I didn't. In my mind I pictured him married to a beautiful Argentinean woman. He and I had had no contact over the past eight years; anything could have happened.

"I came close, Phe," Damon said enigmatically. "Sadly it didn't work out."

Those gray eyes connected with mine again. He was talking about he and I. Dangerous territory.

"It didn't work out because we weren't mature enough to handle an adult relationship," I said. "Adult usually means equal partnership."

"I wanted a wife, kids, a little house complete with picket fence, the whole nine yards."

"And you think I didn't want the same back then?"

His hard gaze swept over me. "You had a funny way of showing it. You chose a career over me, Phe."

Luckily the taxi had pulled into the curb in front of the building. Not too soon as far as I was concerned. I did not like the way this discussion was going. What was the point of resurrecting old hurts?

I stepped around locals sitting in, silently protesting their loss. Several held cardboard signs with photos of the young Maitreya on them. Damon followed on my heels, his backpack slung over one shoulder.

Damon stood right beside me as I made the call. His close proximity made me uneasy. Again it niggled at the back of my mind that he'd come along more to eavesdrop than to render support.

I left my name with the person that picked up and mentioned it was urgent to get a message to Madame Wong. I promised to return to the building in two hours and left the number of the public phone.

"No luck?" Damon asked the moment I hung up.

"A man answered, he said he would pass the message on. You heard what I told him."

"Do you think we even have a shot of collecting our bonus?" Damon asked.

"First let's find out if there's even a statue to work on."

"Good point."

Then arm in arm, we strolled through the streets. We had some time to kill before waiting to see if Madeline would return my call.

As we sauntered down a side street, I spotted a sign that said Brahma's Art & Antiquities. I slowed in front of the shop and stared into a crammed display window. There were a jumble of items for sale but it was the assortment of Buddhas that caught my attention.

"Would you like to go in and browse?" Damon

asked dutifully. I conveniently forgot to tell him
I knew the owner.

"Yes, let's. There are a couple of art history
books I've been looking for. I just might get
lucky."

As we entered, a ruddy Tibetan woman with
braids that touched the hem of her dress stood
talking with a customer. She stuck out a tongue at
us in traditional greeting. There was no sign of
Niall.

The woman, whom I assumed to be Niall's
wife, said to the man, "Yes, you can bring it in.
We'll be happy to take a look and see what it's
worth. You've held on to the piece all this time.
Why sell now?"

The man, who spoke English, answered, "Because, even though I inherited the sculpture,
owning it has meant a lot to me. Now I need the
money and emotions have to be put aside."

"Bring it in two days and my husband will take
a look at it and tell you what it's worth."

I still didn't know what they were talking
about. But the conversation had piqued my
interest. Niall was an experienced art dealer and
it had just been confirmed he had a good eye. He
would most definitely know if an object was authentic or not, and he probably didn't need very
sophisticated tools to make that determination.

Could I trust him with our Maitreya? What's more, could I trust him to keep his mouth shut? No sooner had the thought flashed through my mind than I dismissed it. I'd met Niall Brahma once and only for a brief moment. I knew very little about him. I couldn't risk it.

Damon, the backpack's strap draped over one shoulder, was poking around in corners and removing items that looked as though they might have been there for years. I could tell he was fascinated by the art and antiquities. Catching my eye, he removed an ivory tusk and held it up to his mouth, pretending to charge me. I started laughing.

"Is there something I can help you with?" the woman I presumed to be Mrs. Brahma asked, my rippling laughter gaining her attention.

I introduced myself and Damon followed suit.

Mrs. Brahma seemed delighted to make my acquaintance. "You are the lady my husband wants me to meet. He has invited you to tea."

I nodded. Damon, I could tell, was all ears.

"Niall is on a business trip but will be back tomorrow. Why don't you come to tea the day after tomorrow?"

I smiled and nodded. "That would be lovely."

"Does that invitation include me?" Damon surprised both of us by asking.

"But of course."

What else could she say?

He probably thought cozying up to the proprietor of Brahma's Antiquities might be useful.

If nothing else he'd always been crafty and smart.

But I was smarter.

Chapter 16

We'd been sitting in the waiting room of the Telecom building for about ten minutes when the announcement came.

"Ms. Phoenix Sutherland, there is a call for you."

"Madeline," I hoped.

He followed me to the telephone booth and stood outside hovering. Luckily it was too small to fit both of us.

I picked up the receiver. "Hello."

"Phoenix, is there a problem?"

I rejoiced at hearing Madeline's voice. "Can we speak freely?" I asked.

"You may."

Still, a little voice cautioned me to be careful, reminding me our phone calls could be monitored. Tibet was not the type of country where people spoke freely. Citizens were often thrown in jail for expressing their opinions. And even e-mails coming back and forth were monitored. It seemed logical the same might apply to phone calls.

"Can we meet back at the monastery?" I suggested, changing my mind about free expression.

"I will have to change around a few appointments. But I shall meet you there at four. Will that be a good time?"

"Thank you. I'll be waiting."

I hung up.

"Looks like I'll have 'my friend' in my possession for another few hours," Damon quipped. He eased the backpack gingerly off his shoulder and held it by the handles. "What do we do until then?"

"Let's just head back. We both could use a shower. By the time we clean up, Madeline should be here."

"I've got to figure out what to do about getting those photos developed," Damon said almost to himself.

Eyes peeled for a taxi, we began walking up the street.

I felt a tug on the hem of my denim shirt and turned to see Tashi almost on top of me. He looked forlorn, and for once his bright smile was missing. Tashi held up his pad.

"I have not been able to find you."

Damon shot me a quizzical look.

"He's deaf," I explained. "He can read lips."

"Umm." Damon said, his expression neutral. Given that it was the first time he'd seen Tashi, I gave him a lot of credit. Most reacted to the monk's gruesome appearance with some outward sign of revulsion.

I took the pad from my monk friend and scribbled back, "I've been around. You must not have looked hard enough."

"Where did you meet him?" Damon whispered in my ear.

I explained to him how I'd run into Tashi during one of my sightseeing visits.

"And of all the foreigners in Lhasa he's attached himself to you." Damon sounded skeptical.

I'd thought about that, too. But there were times in this world you just had to trust.

Damon turned away, busy negotiating the fare with the taxi driver. My attention remained on Tashi while I scribbled, "Is everything okay with you?"

His eyes filled with tears.

"Meet me tonight at eleven," he wrote. "I show you something. You bring him with you." He pointed to Damon.

Curiosity prompted me to say, "Where shall we meet?"

"I will meet you in front of your quarters and lead you there."

I thought about that for a moment. I didn't know he knew where I lived. Then again, he had the strange habit of popping up in the most unlikely places.

"Phe," Damon called. "I've got us a driver."

I waved to Tashi and hopped into the back of the cab, mouthing, "See you later."

On the ride back, I turned to Damon. "Where's your backpack? Did you put it in the trunk?"

"What do you mean?" he said. "I handed it to you when you went into the phone booth to take that call."

"No, you did not."

My palms were beginning to sweat.

"I did, Phe." Damon looked down at his ankles as if expecting the bag to be there. He glanced around the backseat as if expecting to find it.

"I saw you with it at the antiquities gallery! After I hung up the phone."

Irritated, I voiced what we both already knew. "You've managed to lose our future."

* * *

Madeline arrived promptly at four. She swept into the outer room in a cloud of Beautiful.

"Phoenix, my darling, what has happened?" She kissed both of my cheeks European style and did the same thing to Damon.

He'd been very quiet ever since he'd lost Maitreya.

"So tell me," Madeline said, her butt perched on one of the stiff straight-back chairs. "How can I help?"

I looked at Damon and he looked back at me. Now how to begin?

"Something happened early this morning," I began.

Madeline crossed one stockinged leg over the other. Her nylons squeaked. She waited patiently for me to go on.

I explained that I'd been awakened by gravel being thrown against my window.

A penciled-in eyebrow arched. When I got to the point in my story where I pretty much stumbled over the cardboard box at the front entrance, Madeline was practically on the edge of her chair.

"What was in the box, Phoenix?"

Again Damon and I exchanged looks. It really didn't matter much now that the statue was no longer in our possession.

"The missing idol," I said.

"Maitreya!"

Madeline seemed dumbfounded. "Someone has gone to great lengths to keep you from working on the statue and then all of a sudden it comes to you."

I nodded.

"But where is it now? The police have been looking everywhere and the town is in an uproar. There are demonstrations all over. I am thinking we must somehow get it back to the building where it was housed." She stood swaying on little pointy heels. "No one is going to believe this story."

I took a deep breath. How could I tell her?

Damon saved me from answering. "I brought the statue into town for safekeeping and somehow managed to lose it. Or someone stole my backpack."

"You did not!" Madeline's cry echoed her disbelief and outrage. "How could you?"

"I'm afraid so. One minute I had my backpack in hand, the next it was gone."

Well, at least he wasn't trying to blame me, claiming that he'd handed it to me, and that it was I who'd lost it.

Madeline was mincing across the room in

those ridiculous high heels. The sleeves of her smart tunic top billowed behind her. "Let me think."

"When I telephoned you, we had the statue in our possession," I explained. "We were calling to get your advice, to figure out how best to let everyone know the statue was found."

"Okay, so Maitreya was in your possession when you made the phone call. Did something happen to distract either of you?" Madeline asked.

I thought about Tashi. His unexpected arrival could be considered a distraction. Come to think of it, it was after leaving him we'd discovered Damon's backpack gone.

"Phe's monk friend showed up," Damon offered.

Madeline's nose wrinkled. "What monk friend?"

"He calls himself Tashi."

I wouldn't have been the least bit surprised if Madeline knew him. She knew everyone there was to know, and then some.

Madeline didn't confirm one way or the other. "How did you meet him?" she asked.

I explained how he'd followed me and kept showing up in the least expected of places.

Her manicured fingers now drummed against her cheeks. I could tell a thought was beginning to percolate in that well-coiffed head of hers.

"And this monk, what does he look like?" she asked.

I described Tashi as kindly as I could. He'd grown on me and I'd become rather fond of him.

"Ah, the artist. The one that was tortured and beaten by the PSB because it was believed he was a staunch supporter of the Dalai Lama. The police used excess force. He lost an eye in the process. The other has almost no peripheral vision. He was almost strangled with their nightsticks. They squashed his voice box in the process."

I was horrified. I'd heard the stories of brutality, but Tashi was visible proof of how horribly a person could be treated.

Damon must have noticed the expression on my face. In an attempt to comfort me, he placed an arm around my shoulders.

"Police brutality happens in the United States, as well, Phe," he said gently.

"At least there is recourse," I cried. "You can file a lawsuit. In the United States if the police are found guilty, they lose their jobs. While it does not make up for the loss of an eye or rendering a person mute, at least there would be some type of monetary settlement."

"Have you considered why the monk would choose you of all people to befriend?" Madeline asked aloud. "There has to be an ulterior motive."

Damon and I exchanged looks. "Why do you say that?" I probed.

"Because Tashi was one of the local artisans slated to restore Maitreya. Then you were hired. That would not make him happy."

I absorbed this cache of information. I'd seen Tashi's work. He was actually quite good, but I'd not thought of him as experienced in restoration.

Madeline, sensing my unspoken question, answered, "It used to be quite common to hire local artisans to do a patch job on antiquities. For one thing it was cheaper than hiring some expert to come in. Mind you, a lot of these repairs were short-lived. That's the reason the historical preservation society came into being.

"During the Cultural Revolution in the mid to late sixties, many temples, monasteries and precious artifacts were destroyed. A quick fix was to get a local artisan to repair a valuable or much-loved treasure. Something was better than nothing."

"We've really never discussed why I was in Lhasa," I said, though that sounded lame. Tashi had to know the reason I was here. He was the one who'd taken me to the gardener. He wasn't exactly dumb. Besides, I stuck out like a sore thumb amongst the paler tourists.

I was tempted to tell Madeline that he'd

asked us to meet him tonight, but something stopped me.

"There are hundreds of tourists in Lhasa. Why select you of all people?" Madeline repeated.

She made a good point. I'd always been one of those people who championed the underdog. I'd felt sorry for Tashi and knew life was not easy for him. I admired the face he put on, and I admired his positive attitude although life must not be easy for him.

"That monk probably has my backpack," Damon muttered, for once looking ruffled.

"What would he hope to gain?" I asked. "We've already been awarded the assignment."

"He'd have, as Andy Warhol said, his fifteen minutes of fame. I'm sure there's a reward offered to anyone finding Maitreya."

"But how would Tashi have known we had him in that bag?"

Madeline nodded sagely. "Didn't you say it yourself? He's been following you."

It hurt like hell to think that he might be a double agent. And that I was stupid and naive enough to fall for it.

Chapter 17

At ten-thirty that evening, after an endless game of hearts, Damon and I said our good-nights to Althea and headed for bed. We'd conferred earlier, agreeing to meet outside the front door at eleven.

Madeline had taken off, promising to contact us the moment she heard anything. By tacit agreement we'd decided not to mention our meeting with Tashi later.

At the appointed hour, Damon and I crept out to the front of the building. I turned on my flashlight and aimed the beam over the surrounding landscaping. No Tashi to be seen.

"Do you think we've been had?" Damon whispered after five minutes went by.

"I'm not sure what that would accomplish."

"By now he should know we're onto him so why would he show up?"

"Assuming he was the one who picked up your backpack," I added.

"True."

A rustling sound came from a nearby alcove. I aimed the beam of the flashlight in that area and spotted Tashi, who held on to the front of his robe with one hand and beckoned us over with the other. Damon used that as an excuse to hold my hand and we picked our way over.

"How do we know we can trust him? This might be a setup," he whispered.

"Forewarned is forearmed," I whispered back.

For about fifteen minutes, we followed the monk, who flitted in and out of one archway or another, and scurried across several courtyards. In the darkness we scrambled up the mountainside, getting to a vantage point where we looked down on the buildings of the monastery. Most were enveloped in darkness. After another five-minute walk, we stopped on the side of what looked to be a crumbling, abandoned building. Nearby there was some sort of outhouse or shed.

Tashi, who'd been ahead of us, looped back

and shooed us over to the side of the shed. My curiosity was brimming over. I aimed my flashlight on the notepad I had thought to bring, and wrote, "Why are we here?"

Tashi removed his hand from under the robe and handed Damon's backpack to him.

In the faint stream of light I registered Damon's complete surprise. He hefted the bag and quickly unzipped it. Satisfied the contents were intact, he eased the straps onto his shoulder.

As he was doing so, Tashi took the notepad from me and wrote, "Your friend forgot the bag on the sidewalk. I spotted it after you got into the taxi. You were already gone."

I wondered if Tashi had opened the backpack and checked the contents. Probably not, or why would he have given it back to us, especially if what Madeline said was true? We were the people who'd taken his job away from him.

"Why are we here?" I wrote.

Tashi's finger rose to his lips. He pressed himself against the wall and motioned to us to do the same then turned off the light. We did the same.

After a few minutes I thought I heard the crunching of gravel nearby. Shadows came out of the blackness and disappeared into a hole in the ground. We leaned against the cement building watching for what felt like an eternity, and getting colder by the moment.

When Damon sneezed, my heart almost stopped. I felt Tashi's panic and sensed his fear. Footsteps crunched closer. Men barked at each other in Tibetan; guards probably. Our only hope was to enter the shed as quickly and quietly as possible. That way we at least stood a chance.

Hugging the walls, I grabbed a handful of Tashi's robe and brought him along with us. Damon and I didn't need to speak. He was already inching his way to where he thought the entrance might be. Tashi wouldn't be a problem. His severed vocal cords took care of any outbursts.

I felt for a door, found it, then quickly grabbed a handle and tugged on it. The footsteps were closer. A dog scratched and whined. The door opened with a screech giving away our hiding place. I scooted in, taking Tashi with me. Damon ducked in behind us.

I slid the interior latch closed and turned on the flashlight, shining it around. It was a storage shed of sorts, holding cement bags and an assortment of building supplies. Crates of stuff were stacked one on top of the other. Two small windows in the rear looked to be sealed tight.

Damon began stacking bags of cement against the inside of the flimsy door. Finding superhuman strength from somewhere, I went over and helped him move more bags. Tashi rolled a wheelbarrow filled with bricks over, obstacles that intruders would have to overcome.

The activity outside picked up. Men were shouting to each other and racing in our direction. The dog was yapping in earnest, as well. Without speaking, Damon and I killed our flashlights. I found Tashi's hand and grabbed it, pulling him toward the rear of the building where I'd memorized the windows to be. I knew Damon could take care of himself.

The door of the shed groaned. Someone had put a shoulder to it. It would only be a matter of time before it splintered.

Damon's words came out in a rush. "I'm going to crouch down. You climb up on my shoulders, Phe." At the same time another crash came from the vicinity of the front door. The wood shuddered. Releasing Tashi's hand, I felt around until I felt sinew and muscle. I hooked one leg over one of Damon's shoulders and the other over the next. I wrapped my arms around his neck. He stood up quickly.

I felt for the window's latch and came up with nothing.

Another crash came from the vicinity of the doorway. I heard wood splinter.

"Hurry, Phe. Their concentration is on that front door."

Using the flashlight, I tapped furiously and shattered the windowpane. Glass showered down on me. My cheeks stung and I felt a warm sticky substance trickle across my face. Blood.

"I'm going to climb out," I whispered. "You and Tashi need to follow quickly."

The creaking, splintering noises coming from the door meant it could give at any time.

"Boost Tashi up," I yelled even as I hurdled through the jagged opening, praying that there would be something to break my fall. I landed on my rump on a hard patch of ground. For a moment I thought I'd broken my tailbone. And I'd lost my flashlight.

Taking several seconds to catch my breath and assess the situation, I realized I'd made it out safe. All the attention was focused on the entrance. No one had thought to monitor the back where the windows were.

A guttural, gasping noise drew my attention to the hole I'd made up above. Then Tashi catapulted out and landed with a thud next to me. Damon quickly followed. Without exchanging a word we began running.

From the shouts coming from inside of the shed I guessed our pursuers had gotten in. It would take them just a few seconds to figure out what had happened. I kept at it, running downhill until my sides ached.

When I stopped to catch my breath, leaning against the sides of an unidentifiable building, it was quiet, too quiet. I raised a hand to my stinging face and removed a sliver of glass.

What did this all mean? What had we uncovered that no one wanted us to see?

Tashi had led us to that area for a reason. I would give it a couple of days until things quieted down then I would return alone. Someone was taking deep breaths right next to me. I stopped breathing. I prepared myself for the confrontation that could follow.

Damon's voice called to me. "Phe, is that you? Are you all right?"

"I'm okay, Damon. But where's Tashi?"

"He made it out of the window fine. I gave him a boost up."

"I saw and heard him land," I confirmed. "Hopefully he ran away."

The silence around indicated we hadn't been followed. Damon, backpack in hand, came toward me. He wasn't going to make the mistake of losing that bag again.

"You and I need to go home, too, Phe," he said, slipping an arm around my waist.

My arm circled his waist, as well. I felt a warm, sticky substance seep through my fingers. It took me a while to figure out what it was.

"You're hurt, " I cried, "bleeding."

Using his free hand, Damon swiped his palm across my cheek. I flinched. "So are you." My face stung and there was some general discomfort, all indicators of glass particles imbedded in my skin.

"You need a doctor," Damon confirmed.

"So do you. But we can't risk anyone seeing us and asking questions."

Damon flipped the switch on his flashlight. "Then let's just go home, Phe. We'll take care of each other."

It sounded like a warm and wonderful promise to me. Half an hour later we were in my cell preparing to clean each other's wounds. I'd found a basin in the sparse kitchen area, filled it with warm water and antiseptic pilfered from the communal bathroom. Damon had found us towels.

"Let me take care of you first, Phe," he said, though I could see his blood-soaked T-shirt and I worried that one of those shards of glass had done some serious internal injury. Damon, after making sure Tashi was out, had probably hurled himself through the jagged opening that was a window, and become impaled a time or two.

He dipped the edges of the towel into the still warm liquid and began swabbing at my face. Although I was in serious pain, I tried not to flinch.

"I need tweezers, I don't suppose you have some?" he asked. To his mind I was definitely not a girlie-girl. All the while his gray eyes gazed at me with compassion and longing. But perhaps the longing was just my imagination. He was probably exhausted and wanted to go to bed.

I gingerly touched my face. "There are splinters imbedded. I can feel them," I said.

"Tweezers, Phe. Do you have them? If not I'm going to have to wake up Althea."

I grabbed his hand. "No, please don't do that. She'll only worry and lecture me. Let me at least check. I should have some somewhere."

I didn't want to talk to anyone about the evening's adventure, not even my best friend. All I wanted to do was find a warm comfortable bed and roll into it.

I had brought the bare minimum of cosmetics with me. I'd tossed the pitifully few items into a zippered bag and stuffed it in the bottom of my duffel bag.

Now I squatted down on the floor and began rifling through the bag impatiently tossing out sneakers, a couple of bras and a Happy Coat that

Madeline had brought me back from Hong Kong as a gift. Finally I found the little plastic bag and wonder of wonders there were tweezers in it. I palmed the tweezers and handed them to Damon.

"This may hurt a bit," he said, his hand under my jaw, tilting my face up.

And it did. But I sat there resolutely letting him pluck every last splinter out of those abrasions. When he was done he dipped the towel into the warm water again and gently patted my face.

"You'll feel better tomorrow. After a good night's sleep," he said. "I can get you a couple of aspirins if you'd like."

I declined his offer of aspirins and turned to him.

"Sit down and let me take care of you."

Damon must have been hurting badly, because there was no bluster or bravado; he just nodded in agreement. With some difficulty he shrugged out of the sticky T-shirt, and muscles bunching, eased onto the straight-back chair.

"Oh, Damon!"

By now the blood had darkened and coagulated around his wounds. Just as I had suspected, with little time to spare, he must have dived headfirst through the broken window. There were deep gashes and cuts where the broken glass had sliced into him. One wound still held a sizable shard. He had to be hurting.

I did my best to extract what pieces of glass I could find and reach with the tweezers. Dipping the towel into the disinfected water, I cleansed his lacerations until the water turned bloody and had to be replaced. All the while I blanked my mind and gave myself a good talking-to. *Think of yourself as a nurse and he a patient. Irrelevant that this man is built like the proverbial brick outhouse or that you've never stopped caring for him.*

Finally I could do no more and I put the water and stained towel aside. Damon, still shirtless, stood. He yawned, showing the first outward signs of tiredness.

"I need sleep, Phe."

"And so do I. Who would have thought we'd get that backpack back?"

"A miracle. Buddha should be thanked." Damon stepped out of his jeans.

It looked as though he planned on sharing my bed again. Tonight I was not adverse to this. After what we'd been through I welcomed his warm body next to mine. By some tacit agreement there would be no sex. We were both too physically exhausted and shaken up to even think of such a thing. This would be about providing emotional comfort and spiritual support.

"Maybe you should take Maitreya out of your

backpack," I suggested, yawning, and still fully clothed, slid under the covers.

Damon picked up the bag and brought it to bed with him. He set it down at our feet. "We'll leave it until tomorrow. I'm too exhausted to even look."

Pulling me up against him, he settled in next to me.

"Thank you for taking such good care of me, Phe," he said. "I've missed your touch."

I'd missed him, too.

Chapter 18

When my eyes popped open the following morning, I spotted the folded slip of paper shoved under the door. Still groggy with sleep, I rolled over and reached out an arm. Damon had left me.

I was wide-awake now, and realizing that both he and his backpack were gone.

Wounds still aching and limbs sore, I crept across the stone floor and headed for the bathroom. On the way out, I bent over and palmed the note.

I didn't recognize the handwriting. After scanning the note, I debated whether it was a hoax or not.

I was being asked to meet Yuyi, the gardener, on the main steps in front of the Tshomchen. I assumed he'd gotten some English-speaking person to write on his behalf.

He'd picked a rather well-traveled area, so I didn't think anything *too* underhanded was afoot. The pilgrims frequented that location. It was where they went to make offerings to the Bodhisattva of Wisdom.

I had to go. I thought about bringing Althea or Damon along with me, but I couldn't honestly say I trusted my ex. I decided against Damon. Althea I couldn't bring along, either; arriving with another woman might not go over well.

My thoughts turned to Tashi. He would have been the ideal companion to accompany me. While he did not speak, he had an incredible comprehension of the English language, and he knew Yuyi.

I hoped Tashi had made it home without further incident. I found a pair of jeans and a reasonably clean sweater and scrambled into them. Armed with my map of the grounds, I dashed from the building without running into a soul.

Not very good at reading maps, I floundered. The thought occurred if I tagged along behind one of the pilgrims I would eventually get there. The Manjushri Temple behind the Tshomchen was for them a definite draw.

I found several who spoke English, asked where they were heading, and when I got the answer I wanted, followed their path.

By the time I arrived at the appointed meeting place I was at least a half an hour late. Tourists were there in droves and had pretty much taken over. Some sat on the steps, faces tilted to the sun, others snapped pictures or clutched minicamcorders and tried to convince a local to pose for them. I plopped down on a step, my eyes peeled for the gardener, hoping he had not given up. Around me there was a steady flow of different languages.

Fifteen minutes later I was still seated there. By then I had come to the conclusion I'd either been led on a wild-goose chase or he'd gotten fed up and left. I played back the events leading me here. How would Yuyi have gotten a note pushed under my door?

Standing, I stretched, and removed my sunglasses. I looked around to see if anyone remotely resembling him was anywhere in the vicinity. Crowded as the area had become, there was always the possibility that he might not have seen me.

I had just about given up on him when I saw a short man hovering in the area of the rock gardens. He was with a heavier man and they were scanning the surrounding areas looking for something or someone. I decided to walk in that direction.

Yuyi recognized me when I was almost on top of him and elbowed his friend. The heavyset man acknowledged me with a nod.

"Good morning, Miss Sutherland."

The correctness of his English surprised me.

"Good morning," I replied.

"We were not certain you would get the message. My friend here—" he referred to Yuyi "—gave it to one of the dining-room staff to pass on to you. We are glad that you have come."

I smiled at Yuyi. He did not smile back.

"What is it you want with me?" I asked, and waited for his friend to interpret.

"He wants you to come home with him."

"What?"

"His brother does not have long to live. He wants to speak with you," the interpreter explained.

"But how does he know me? We've never met."

"He knows of you." I had still not been formally introduced. "Khalish used to do repairs and a bit of masonry at the temples. In your country you would call him a laborer. He speaks very little English. If you are agreeable, I'll come along with you and I can help translate."

"I'm still not understanding what is wanted of me."

"You will soon find out. I am a family friend and I have been asked to help with the translation."

"Okay, I will go, but I did tell my friends I was meeting you. They are expecting me back within the hour." The last was added in the event I was about to conveniently disappear.

We made a strange trio as I walked with them to an area where a battered minivan was parked. The family friend, whose name I still didn't know, climbed into the driver's seat. In a short while things started to look a little familiar, and we pulled up in front of the hovel that Tashi had led me to several days back.

As we entered a small courtyard, I could smell incense coming from the house's interior. I also heard chanting and a woman's loud wails.

"His wife," my driver explained.

Yuyi led the way inside the house that smelled of pungent herbs and balm. The smell of death and a rapidly decaying body mingled with cooking. I entered a tiny room that needed ventilation. Lying on a pallet on the floor was a skeletal body that looked as if it was ready for embalming.

Forcing myself to look at the still figure swaddled in blankets, I felt saddened. The man's face, already a death mask, was the color of uncooked liver and every inch of exposed flesh was covered in spots. I didn't know what leprosy looked like, but I sure wanted to retch.

"You will need to come closer, he can barely speak," the interpreter said, placing a hand on the small of my back and giving me a gentle nudge forward.

Conscious of the keening woman standing in the doorway, I made my legs move. I approached the still form hoping that my stomach would not betray me. The smells were cloying and much stronger closer up.

Yuyi fitted himself into a corner. It remained eerily quiet except for the soft gurgling sounds coming from the emaciated body. Even the crying wife was now silent.

The interpreter broke the silence. "Kneel down and place your ear to his mouth."

I found that idea most revolting, but how could I not? Thankfully I had not eaten. If I embarrassed myself there would be little to regurgitate. Not wanting to offend, rather than placing a hand over my nose and mouth, I held my breath and got to my knees, then allowed myself to slowly exhale.

The wife knelt on the other side of the bed. She held a baby's bottle with a clear liquid in one hand, and what looked to be a wad of cotton in the other.

After moistening the cotton, she swabbed at the emaciated man's lips then inserted the nipple of the bottle.

I felt like a voyeur witnessing what only close family members should be privy to.

The man who'd driven us now got down on his knees next to me. "Khalish," he said, gently shaking the man, and speaking softly first in Tibetan then English. "Khalish, the American woman is here."

Gurgle. Gurgle. The bottle hung from his lifeless lips. Had he gone into some kind of semicoma?

The friend and Yuyi now conversed in rapid Tibetan. The interpreter turned back to me. "Let me try my best to explain why you are present. This man, Khalish, the brother of Yuyi, has been working at a vault in the temple."

Still not sure where this was going, I nodded. "Yes, you did say he was a laborer."

"Khalish is feeling guilty because he has stolen something."

What in the world did that have to do with me? I was hardly mother confessor, since arriving in Tibet I had stolen a man's vehicle. Even worse I had destroyed it. And I hadn't made reparations because I still didn't know whether the owner was alive or dead.

"What has he stolen?" It seemed the logical thing to ask.

Yuyi and his friend exchanged looks. Several lengthy beats went by. "A statue," the neighbor finally said. "A valuable idol that is being looked for."

My reaction was visible as my lower jaw flapped open. How could a man on his deathbed and hardly in any shape to walk, steal anything?

I'd been skeptical about the story of Damon setting the backpack down and forgetting about it. He'd guarded that bag as if he were one of the protector statues at the Three Ages Chapel.

"Suppose you explain it to me," I said. "I'm just not getting it."

Another exchange in Tibetan followed. There seemed to be some sort of argument as the neighbor and Yuyi went back and forth.

The interpreter switched to English. "One of Khalish's jobs has been to move crates back and forth. He does as he is told and seldom asks questions. When he was well he had an evening job at the vault where many artisans create statues."

The hair raised on my arms. "What kinds of statues?"

"I am coming to that."

"Go on."

"These were, how do you say, ah, yes, reproductions of the Buddhas. At first Khalish did not think anything of it. He would go to the vault under supervision to pick up a crate or deliver one. Then things eased up as they grew more comfortable with him. He was sent alone and he began to wonder why it was always at night. He began recognizing familiar faces. People whose pictures were in the newspaper."

I was alert.

"As you can tell, this is a very poor family," the friend said, continuing. "They have practically nothing. Khalish sees the statues coming and going. He figures out that the valuable ones are being copied. He thinks they will never know the difference if one of the originals disappears. So when he is asked to remove a crate from the vault and take it to a storage unit, he gives it to Yuyi instead."

"And Yuyi decides to hide the crate on the grounds until he can dispose of it?"

"You are a bright lady. Then his gardener friends come along as he is just burying the box. He must pretend that he has discovered this object. They call the boss and the rest, as you say, is history."

I was still trying to figure out why I had been chosen to hear this confession.

By some divine providence the ill man's eyes

popped open. His eyeballs were yellow and pupils dilated. He opened his mouth, releasing a string of gibberish.

My interpreter appeared to be listening carefully.

"What does the doctor say about Khalish's condition?" I asked. I hoped his affliction wasn't contagious.

"He will most likely die. He knows that. We have been expecting it, and that is one of the reasons you are here. He heard you were hired to restore the statue."

"Why is that?" I asked, and needed to know. "Why would he care about me?"

The neighbor began talking in earnest with Yuyi. I gathered my concerns were being translated.

"Yuyi noticed you were friends with the monk. He thinks you should not trust him. He also thinks the idol is cursed. One of the men who comes to the vault has a sick wife. Another one has just been killed in a car accident."

Liu Bangfu. Xiong Jing. Just as I thought.

"I appreciate Yuyi's concern," I said. "But why am I here? What is it that he wants from me?"

"He thinks his brother will die peacefully if you can make the statue whole again. That is why he returned it to you."

Yuyi had been the one to place the idol on the convent's doorstep. He and his dying brother must have managed to steal the statue a second time; that's why the crate had been empty. They were superstitious and needed absolution. If I restored the statue the curse would go away.

Too much information to process right now, but certainly a lot to think about. My suspicions were confirmed. From the very beginning I'd thought there was something off about the idol and I was right.

Maitreya, whose name meant "loving kindness," was considered the Universal Christ and said to arrive when the world was in turmoil. He was to judge the wicked and save the righteous. A "kind friend" did not hurt people.

Bhaisajyaguru, on the other hand, was the Buddha of Medicine. As a healer he was gifted with quelling disease and lengthening life. He defended the health of the faithful, the key word being *faithful*. One of the twelve vows he'd made was to reinforce all in observing ethics. If he was being used for unethical practices then the reverse could happen. Illness could result.

"The Healer" was lapis lazuli in color and in his right hand he held a plant with medicinal properties. I remembered the missing hand of the Buddha and the greenish-blue hue to the yellow.

If someone had painted yellow over blue then that would make green.

I needed to get back to the monastery and get my hands on Maitreya. I wanted to look at that lopped-off hand.

I needed to examine his color.

Chapter 19

"You've been gone a long time, Phe," Damon greeted me as I dashed into the convent. "I was starting to worry."

"You've been here the whole day?" I asked. I dodged his question, sweet and caring as it was.

"No, I went into town to see what I could do about developing those photographs."

My heart palpitated. Had he found something he was willing to share? "And?" I said expectantly. "Were you able to?"

We were standing in the vestibule while this conversation took place. Both of us seemed reluctant to venture a step farther.

"Yes. Then I went back to that art gallery and poked around a bit. The owner was there. What did you do?"

"I wandered about for a while trying to find Tashi. I was worried about him. Strange he hasn't tried to contact me."

"He's fine."

How could Damon know that?

And what, if anything, had shown up when he'd developed those photographs?

"We need to do something about that statue," I said instead. "I guess I should call Madeline again and let her know it was returned."

Damon's fingers circled my wrist. We stood inches from each other. His touch had me quivering but I stood my ground. Lowering his voice, he said, "I don't have the statue, Phe."

"What do you mean? You don't have Maitreya? I saw Tashi give your backpack to you."

"But that's just it. Remember the statue was wrapped in a towel. I never unwrapped the towel to verify the contents. I took it at face value. When I opened the bag later and really looked, a substitute had been put in his place."

Was he lying to me? Playing me for a fool? More angry at myself than him, I decided to be very direct.

"What was in the backpack, Damon? Just give it to me straight."

"The heart of a goat."

I forced myself to ask, "What did you do with this heart?"

"Disposed of it, of course."

I kept my eyes on his face, looking for signs of shiftiness.

"Phe, I've been thinking about it and what it all means. *Ra* is the word for goat in Tibetan. Lhasa a long time ago was called Rasa. There's a statue of a goat inside the Jokhang in the chapel of Maitreya. A local person, this thief, is sending you a warning. He considers himself the heart of Lhasa and the protector of Maitreya. You are the interloper. You must go."

While it did seem a bit over the top, Damon's words had some merit to them. But was he telling me the truth? He had wanted to get hold of the statue of Maitreya from the very beginning. Now that we suspected the idol might be a fraud, what use would he have for it? He'd wanted Maitreya for the Dalai Lama.

Bhaisajyaguru, the Medicine Buddha, one of the trio was a healer, and not a savior of the people. There was some monetary value associated with him. The Damon I knew had never been about money.

I tugged out of his reach. "I'm exhausted, I have to take a nap." My head was whirling.

"Phe, don't you want to hear about my findings? The photos I developed?" He followed me down the hallway.

I was on overload, processing too much information and trying to make sense of it. I stopped and in a protective gesture, folded my arms across my chest.

"Sure, why not."

"I'm fairly certain that statue's not Maitreya," he said, confirming what I pretty much knew. "I was able to determine the right hand's been purposely hacked off and the idol painted over. I'm thinking it's the Medicine Buddha that someone has been trying to pass off as Maitreya."

I spoke my thoughts out loud. "But why? This would mean the statue which disappeared on my father's watch was not the real deal. Dad might have been set up. How would the idol have mysteriously made its way back to Tibet?"

Damon shook his head. "The whole thing makes no sense to me."

But it was beginning to make sense to me. If someone was replicating statues, then they were doing so for their own gain. They must be selling them to someone for a good price. If everyone thought the statue was stolen while in the United States no one would think to look for it in Tibet.

Now I was more convinced than ever to see this through. I would go to the secluded area again tonight. I would find a way to gain access to that vault where Khalish, the laborer, had worked.

"I have to take a nap," I said. "After last night I'm just too fried to think. Please don't wake me if I sleep through dinner. Tell Althea I'll catch up with her tomorrow."

Damon gazed at me with some concern, his voice was gentle when he spoke. "A nap's probably a good idea, Phe. You've been through a lot. I'd offer to join you but I'm going to find a place to meditate. I need to think this whole bizarre situation through."

With that we parted company.

I did manage to sleep. Aided by my alarm clock, I awoke after dark, dug through my personal things, found a box of crackers and a can of tuna stashed in the event of an emergency, and scoffed it down. I hadn't eaten all day.

Then I scribbled a note about my whereabouts, and dressed in the native outfit that Althea had purchased and given to me. In the daylight I might not pass as a local, but at night, I stood a good chance.

Grabbing my flashlight, the map I had difficulty reading and the matches used to light candles and incense, I headed out, stopping first to slide the note under Althea's door.

My plan was to get back to the area that Tashi had taken us to last night. I wanted to be there before any activity started. I was well aware that I risked discovery; after last evening's events, security was probably crawling all over the place.

Operating primarily from memory, I darted between buildings and across courtyards, trudging up the mountainside, getting disoriented then reorienting myself. Finally I came to an area that seemed familiar.

My eyes soon adjusted to the darkness. I was certain I'd come to the abandoned building and the outhouse off to the side. Hoping to give myself an advantage, I'd arrived earlier than the previous evening. There didn't seem to be much activity.

A dog growled and my heart leaped into my mouth then settled. Rounding the corner, I spotted a powerful beast tied to a post. The ruckus roused a guard, who began circling the area. He untied the dog and took it with him, heading off in the opposite direction. I needed something to distract them.

On tiptoe, I doubled back, listening to see if I was being followed. The dog continued to howl and the guard yelled at him. A plan had begun to form.

I headed for where I thought enough flammable brush might be, squatted down, reached into my pocket and removed the map and matches. Setting the pile on the ground, I started a fire. I then kicked the entire blazing bundle into a pile of debris. I returned to the area I'd left and waited.

After silently poking around, I discovered the main building had a crumbling staircase. Darting behind several pillars, I carefully made my way over. I couldn't tell whether the fire had ignited or fizzled, but I did hear the dog howling and the guard crunching about. Finally I smelled smoke. The guard shouted and, taking the dog with him, he scrambled off in that direction.

I was fairly certain he was the only one around. Now would be my opportunity to act while he was distracted. Last evening I'd seen people literally coming and going into a hole in the ground. There must be a trapdoor somewhere.

I tried my best to memorize where that area was. I couldn't risk turning my flashlight on just in case I was mistaken and there were more guards on the grounds. But I was willing to risk lighting a match, just to get my bearings. Holding my breath, I stepped from under the staircase. All was silent. I squinted into the darkness and ignited a match.

In the illumination I saw dirt, gravel and materials that had been left over from an earlier or maybe current attempt at repairs. No sign of a door anywhere. I blew the match out before it burned my fingers.

Stupid! I thudded a closed fist against my forehead. No one would leave an entry exposed, especially if there was something unorthodox going on. I decided I would walk in the direction of the building supplies. At the very least it would provide me with a place to hide should the guard come back unexpectedly.

Rather than push my luck, I decided to wait before I lit another match. I'd visualized the area where I needed to be, and I slowly made my way over in the dark. Proud of myself that things were going so well, I made it to the stack of wood and materials and crouched down behind them.

A rough palm clamped over my mouth. The other wrapped itself around my waist and hoisted me to my feet.

"Gotcha," a New York voice said in my ear.

The crackers and tuna I'd eaten earlier pinged in my stomach and jockeyed to get out. I knew that voice. It shouted Bronx.

Angry, I bit into the flesh of the inner palm.

"Stop being difficult, Phe, and I'll put you down. Nice outfit. You've gone native I see."

Damon set me back on my feet but left his palm clamped over my mouth. At the same time we both heard a crunching sound signifying the guard was back or a new person had entered the picture. Damon whispered in my ear, "I'm going to remove my hand from your mouth, Phe. If you scream we're both dead people."

What choice did I have? If he was in with these people I was done for anyway and if he was not, I would be giving away our hiding place. It was a no-win situation all around.

I could smell smoke, stronger now. The guard called to this second person, who quickly changed direction, and began running to help put out the fire, I assumed. Damon took his hand off my mouth. I exhaled deeply, drinking in the cool night air.

Keeping my voice low, I snapped, "Why are you here?"

"The same reason you are." He smartly side-stepped the question.

Scurrying sounds came from someplace at our feet. Damon flicked on his flashlight, aiming the rays at the base of the stack of materials we hid behind. "Damn," he announced. At the same time something that looked to be about the size of a cat bounded across his foot. I put my fist in my mouth to prevent the scream that tore out.

I heard his low chuckle.

"You see any signs of building or repair?" he whispered when he'd stopped. "Those materials are too organized. It's as if each piece of wood and brick has an arranged spot. Even the bags of cement are strategically placed."

"And you're thinking…" I whispered back.

"I'm thinking they're covering up something."

"You look. I'm not risking rats," I said to him emphatically.

"You take on grown men yet you're afraid of rats."

"Only the four-legged kind."

He knew better than to laugh.

"Keep watch," Damon said, getting down on his knees and methodically starting to move planks of wood and rubble aside. More rats scuttled. Fist in my mouth, I hopped up and down as quietly as I could.

"I found something," Damon mumbled just loud enough for me to hear.

"What?"

"Come closer."

I was afraid to turn on my flashlight for fear of discovery. Instead I lit a match. In the flickering light, I registered what he was showing me with quiet excitement. Under the bags of cement and timber was a door set flat into the ground.

"I'm going down," I said without giving it another thought.

"And I'm coming with you. We need to move quickly."

In the distance gravel shifted. Voices came at us, the sounds of more people arriving. It was now or never.

Damon heaved the door open, revealing a big black hole. He shone his flashlight into the opening, illuminating what looked to be rungs leading down.

"Ladies first," he said standing aside. "I'll be right behind you."

I didn't think, just lowered myself into the gaping opening and placed a foot on the first rung. I heard Damon follow me and heard him click the overhead trapdoor shut. If this was our only access and exit we could be in trouble.

I felt for the next rung, then the next, and the next, stepping carefully and clinging to the sides of the rough walls. I just kept lowering myself down, resigned to not having fingernails but bleeding stubs.

Our climb into hell seemed to go on forever. I missed a rung, faltered and swung from the wall. I felt myself falling. A scream ripped out. Eventually I landed on my tailbone on the hard floor.

Enveloped in darkness, and aching from the impact, I waited to be discovered. Silence. No one around.

Finally footsteps and ragged breathing in my ear. "Are you hurt, *chica?*"

Damon had found me. He lifted me to my feet then set me down. I was able to support my weight, nothing was broken. He flicked on his flashlight and shone it around.

The cavernous room we were in seemed to be some kind of manufacturing area. Statues surrounded us in various stages of production. Primitive sculpturing tools and basins of hardening clay and cement sat on workstations. On the far side of the room were packing crates.

We silently made our way over to the crates, easing ourselves behind the two tallest ones.

"Might as well get comfortable and wait. Kill the light, Damon," I whispered.

Instead of listening to me, he let the beam play on the walls around us.

"There's got to be another way out. No way could anyone get those crates up that steep staircase. "Aha. There it is."

I turned to see what he was looking at. He pointed at a wall panel that didn't seem to butt up evenly against the adjoining wall. "I bet you anything," he said, "that panel slides."

I heard the sound of the overhead trapdoor opening at the same time he did.

"Kill the light, we've got company."

My finger raised to my lip. He snapped off the flashlight and we pressed ourselves against the crate and waited.

It sounded like a herd of elephants were stampeding. People were scrambling down the rungs and into the vault. The clanging and banging made me think they might be carrying their work tools with them.

Someone triggered a switch and the area became flooded with light. I gazed around the room, now getting a clearer view. I noted the assembly line set up and the Buddhas in various stages of development.

Workmen were now taking their stations and the panel on the far side of the room slid open. Out stepped Liu Bangfu, Kalon Nyandek, the government official I'd met at the uncrating, and Niall Brahma, the art dealer.

My instincts had been right!

As the men walked the room, stopping to ask a question or two of the artisans, I spotted a face that was familiar. Sadness, confusion and anger flooded me.

Tashi.

Chapter 20

The Maitreya, rather Bhaisajyaguru with its bluish-green hue, sat on the workstation in front of Tashi. Next to the statue's body lay the severed hand, herbal plant and all.

The two government officials, accompanied by Niall, were now standing in front of Tashi's station. Niall scooped up the Medicine Buddha while the two officials barked something at the monk. Liu Bangfu after a few seconds punched the monk in the face.

Indeed this was a well-oiled operation. The replicas being made would replace a more valuable piece. The authentic statues would most likely be sold to collectors. And this negotiation probably took place through an art dealer. Disguised in some form, the statues would then be sent out of the country.

I also remembered a snippet of conversation around that deathbed. There'd been talk of Yuyi and Khalish cutting a deal with a gallery owner in town. It must have been Niall. Befriending me had been a calculated move on his part. He'd probably done so to see what I knew.

Damon, the person I'd least trusted, had turned out to be a friend. Whereas Tashi, who had befriended me, even leading me to this area, was working for the enemy.

And crooks were exactly what Liu Bangfu and Kalon Nyandek had turned out to be. These were unscrupulous people who would very easily kill someone if they got in their way.

More men were beginning to arrive. They scrambled down into the abyss with ease. A man who looked to be the foreman began a conversation with Liu Bangfu. Afterward he shouted instructions to two sturdy men.

The men, who were built like miniature tree trunks, got dollies from a corner. They dragged or kicked them across the room directly toward the crates where we were hidden.

"They're coming toward us," I whispered. "I'm not going down without a fight."

"I'll be your backup," Damon said, feet wide apart and knees slightly bent. I didn't have time to give voice to my surprise.

Somewhere along the way Damon had learned karate-jitsu. He assumed the perfect Horse Stance.

Putting most of my weight on my front foot and setting the other leg back, I got into the Front Stance. We might be outnumbered, but if guns weren't involved we should be able to give as good as we got, maybe even better.

Everything began happening quickly. One crate got moved and placed on a dolly, then another. The laborers conversed amongst themselves as they hefted one box and then the other. When they were down to maybe six, they began easing them across the room. They pushed the paneling and set the crates into the open space. Damon and I were still behind a protective barrier. For now.

All of a sudden a booming voice amplified by a megaphone penetrated the night. Someone snapped off the light and the place plunged into darkness. The voice continuing in Tibetan rang out in authority. Panic was now a palpable thing around us. The trapdoor overhead banged open and a searchlight illuminated the floor.

People began scrambling for cover. Liu Bangfu and Kalon Nyandek raced toward the sliding wall. Another barked order stopped them. Niall continued running, Bhaisajyaguru in hand. A shot rang out. He pitched forward but didn't drop the statue in his hand.

Officers, dozens of them, guns drawn, began descending the ladder. They grouped together in the center of the room, their guns trained on the artisans. For a brief second they faltered as the PSB recognized their Minister of Religion and Culture and the other government official. But the officers soon rallied. They quickly surrounded the men and began cuffing them, including Niall, who'd been shot in the leg.

A female voice I recognized came through the megaphone. "Phoenix, are you down there?"

Madeline Wong to the rescue again. Althea must have called her after reading my note.

Leaving the safety of the crates, I stepped forward, arms above my head as if I were surrendering. Damon followed suit. I trusted that Madeline was at a vantage point to see both of us.

"The chief of police is with me," she announced through the megaphone. "So is your friend Althea."

The artisans were now all being herded into a group, Tashi amongst them. He must have seen me by now but I could not bring myself to look at him.

The room slowly emptied as the artists, ministers and Niall were led off. Another team of officers arrived and began cordoning off the area; some gathered evidence.

When Madeline and Althea came through the paneled area, Damon pointed to the opening.

"There are crates back there," he said. "Some of them quite large."

Madeline translated Damon's words and several of the officers charged into the opening.

Finally there was nothing else for us to do but go to the PSB station and fill out statements. Althea, although we told her it was not necessary, insisted on accompanying us. There, with the aid of an interpreter, we completed our business.

After thanking Madeline profusely for her help, and promising to name my firstborn after her, I got into the car she had waiting.

"Tomorrow I will send another car for you," she said. "We will have lunch and talk about this." She slid into her own chauffeured vehicle. "Tomorrow we may even have a few chuckles."

We watched her drive away.

I laid my head on Damon's shoulder and closed my eyes. I vaguely remembered arriving back at my room and being put to bed.

I must have slept the sleep of the dead because the next thing I remembered was awakening to a pounding on my door.

Damon said the moment I opened the door, "We have to meet at the Minister of External Affairs' office. A representative from the United States embassy will be meeting us there. Madeline's car will pick us up to take us to that lunch. You've got fifteen minutes to get ready, Phe." He was already fully dressed.

Skipping a shower, I threw on the most presentable thing I had. I found a car waiting to take us to the Minister of External Affairs' office, housed in the same temporary quarters as Liu Bangfu's had been.

The conference room we were ushered into was filled with people. I was surprised to find Madeline there. She winked at me but said nothing.

After we were seated, a polished Chinese gentleman clad in a well-tailored navy suit introduced himself as Phillip Wong, Minister of External Affairs. The chief of police was amongst the seated people. Today he was dressed in civilian clothes.

Another man rose as I entered; he introduced himself as Jonathan Coombs and handed me a card. He was from the United States embassy.

The others in the room I guessed to be plain-clothes public security staff.

Phillip Wong opened the conversation. "We want to thank you for uncovering a criminal operation," he said. "It is an embarrassing situation for the People's Republic of China to discover that two of their own, officials considered to be trustworthy, were involved in such a mess. Both men have confessed to their wrongdoings and have been charged."

"What have they confessed to?" I asked.

"Misappropriating funds, replicating statues and selling the originals for their own gain. Ever since the 1980s, Tibet has made a concerted effort to restore its antiquities, temples, buildings and artifacts. Our historical preservation society has raised funds and received grants from all over the world. These funds allow us to hire experts like you to come in to restore and preserve our history."

"So what you're saying is that grant money was not utilized in the manner it was supposed to be?"

"That's right," Jonathan Coombs answered. "The ex-Minister of Religion and Culture, aided by the deceased Xiong Jing, hired a number of local artisans cheaply. He paid them poorly and the rest went into his pocket. He also had something worked out with Mr. Brahma to sell the authentic idols to private collectors. The dealer got a nice cut and so did our ex-Minister of Culture and his friend, Xiong Jing, as did Kalon Nyandek. Jing was killed because they thought he was confiding in you. By the way, Liu Bangfu's wife died this morning. He is inconsolable."

I'd never met the woman. Still she'd been an innocent in all of this as far as I knew. I was saddened.

"What about the monk, Tashi? How did he come into play?" I asked.

"He was one of the misused artisans and very good at what he did. He would disguise the real statues so that they could be smuggled out of the country."

"But he befriended me. It was he who led me to the spot where they were replicating idols," I said, wondering why I still cared.

Tashi was a double agent, I reminded myself. He'd pretended to be on our side, just enough to make us feel we were making progress, but really a part of the dirty scheme.

"He's been offered a reduced sentence," Wong said. "To use the Western expression, he sang. He told us that our minister, ex that is, had reneged on the agreed salary, small amount that it was. He then became angry. This is a man who could barely feed himself. He thought you were a nice lady."

Fat good that did.

"How does the gardener, Yuyi, fit into this?" I asked.

"Gardener?" John Coombs said. "You mean the one that thought he found Maitreya? He has nothing to do with this."

I wisely kept my mouth shut on that point. For all that I knew Khalish was probably dead and vulture droppings by now. May he rest in peace. Amen.

"So what I'm hearing you say is that by virtue of my being hired, I was a threat. Your ex-Minister of Religion and Culture couldn't risk being found out. He was the one who hired people to follow me and try to convince me to go home. Like the pickpocket."

"Exactly," the Minister of External Affairs said. "And when that didn't work, they got desperate and resorted to bombings. Liu Bangfu had been lobbying for new offices all along. He got them when he hired someone to help demolish that old building."

"And he took innocent people's lives along the way." I couldn't help my outburst.

"It is an honor to die in some parts of the world," Jonathan Coombs said, his expression neutral.

"What will happen now?" I asked. "We've been here going on three weeks. We were given a deadline to restore Maitreya and we were told we'd receive a bonus. It's now been confirmed the statue is Bhaisajyaguru. This is the same statue reputedly stolen while on loan to a museum in the United States. Knowing what we know now, that statue never left Tibet."

Phillip Wong cleared his throat. "Yet another embarrassment for our government. On behalf of the People's Republic of China, I must apologize to you. A public apology will be issued to the United States. You will receive your bonus, plus some. My government has said they will be honored if you stay to restore and reconstruct the Medicine Buddha. Perhaps one day we will find his mates, Manjushri and Maitreya, and you will work on them, also. What do you say, Ms. Sutherland?"

I glanced at Damon and Althea. Both nodded.

"I speak on behalf of us all," I said. "We would be delighted to restore Bhaisajyaguru."

"Well, now that that's decided," Madeline said, "and my brother-in-law has cleared that all up, we'll need to run along to our lunch appointment." She stood, signaling the meeting was over, at least as far as she was concerned.

I thanked Phillip Wong, Madeline's brother-in-law, and John Coombs. I shook their hands, as did Damon and Althea. Then I followed Madeline's mincing steps out to the car.

It was finally over with. If we worked like dogs, in a month or so we could be home.

More important, I'd achieved what I'd come for. I'd made my father whole.

Chapter 21

"Happy Birthday, Dad!" I celebrated, raising my glass in a toast.

The guests at my father's party quickly followed suit.

It was a month and a half later and Tibet seemed so far removed from the daily grind of New York. Even so, I was grateful to be back in the United States.

I rolled the huge chocolate cake into the living room. The cake had been created especially to honor my dad, and expressly according to my instructions. The baker had created a Buddha; the left hand a begging bowl, the right a medicinal plant.

He'd gone a little overboard using yellow M&M's for the eyes, mouth and belly button, and using green for the plant. The cake drew a chuckle from the guests fortifying themselves with the champagne being served.

Aunt Estelle hurried toward me, relieving me of the cart transporting the cake. She parked it on the side of the dining-room table, and as efficient as always, produced matches. She quickly lit the sparklers topping the cake.

Now I tried to blend in with the wall while surreptitiously looking around the room. People spilled from the dining room into the kitchen and out to the living room again.

It was a varied assortment of friends, relatives and colleagues. Even my brothers came. All here to celebrate my father's sixtieth birthday, improved health and two-book deal he'd signed with a major publisher. I was ecstatic for him. It had been a long road getting here.

Dad looked wonderful. He was almost back to his old self. I watched him laugh and joke with his guests. At peace with himself, he'd gained back most of the weight he'd lost during those dark days.

His pecan-colored skin had a glow to it now

and his eyes held an intelligent sparkle in their depths. The doctor attributed the change to the new medication he'd been given, but I knew better. No medication could work as well as having your name cleared.

There had been no better prescription for my dad than finding out that the real Bhaisajyaguru had never been sent to the United States. Once that news broke, all the major papers had jumped on the story. Overnight, Thomas Sutherland had become a victim of circumstance, a man who'd been framed. He'd been besieged with offers to come aboard and serve as curator at some of the more prestigious museums the city had to offer. He'd turned them all down.

Instead, my dad had accepted a position on the board of directors of the same museum where he'd been forced to resign. He'd decided his days of being a curator, as rewarding as they once were, were now over. At his age he no longer wanted that responsibility or stress.

These last few weeks he'd spent fielding calls. It seemed everyone wanted a piece of him. He'd been invited on television and radio shows, and had even been asked by a couple of universities to lecture.

I found it interesting that those who had vilified him before, now lauded his past accomplishments and conveniently forgot how they publicized his earlier fall from grace.

"Speech! Speech! Speech!" a guest shouted.

"Yes, speech!"

The chant slowly began with others picking it up.

A hired waiter began making the rounds topping off champagne glasses. My father declined and Aunt Estelle surreptitiously filled my dad's glass with the ginger ale he'd been drinking. Alcohol and the powerful medications he was now on were not a good mix.

The room quieted as everyone waited for my father to speak. I could tell he was humbled by the number of people who'd poured into my aunt Estelle's brownstone in Morningside, a tony Harlem address. All four floors swarmed with people, most of whom were now on the second floor waiting for the cake to be cut.

Dad raised his glass and those there to celebrate with him followed.

"I am honored and gratified that you are here to share this milestone of my life," he said in the deep baritone I loved so much. "It is not every day one turns sixty."

"You can say that again," one of my dad's cronies called from the back of the room. "And you don't look a day over forty."

A slight exaggeration really, although Dad, with his cropped gray hair and virtually unlined face, did look good for his age.

Dad spoke over the crowd's laughter, "And it is not every day one gets the opportunity to pursue a dream. Who would have thought that out of adversity would come opportunity. Now I am contracted to write two books about subjects that are near and dear to me—art, antiquities and history."

Another round of applause broke out.

My brothers converged on me. Two placed a protective arm around my waist. I was five foot nine but they towered over me. I was still considered the "squirt."

"He looks and sounds great, doesn't he?" Luke, the oldest, whispered.

Blinking away tears, I nodded. "Yes, I am so proud of him."

There was a lot to be proud of. My dad had rallied and had barely been bitter when the news broke. The Chinese government, eating crow, had been forced to admit that the real Bhaisajyaguru was never sent to the United States. Instead, a replica had been sent in its place, even though it had arrived with authenticity papers attached.

Where my dad could be faulted was for not having the statue authenticated again. But who would have thought to do so? The arrangements had been made through the governments of the respective countries. How would anyone guess the Tibetan Minister of Religion and Culture, Liu Banfu, was a crook? My father, the curator, had accepted the statue at face value and assumed all was on the up-and-up.

Dad was done with his speech. The applause was deafening. His colleagues surrounded him, patting him on the back, seeking his advice on some collectible or antiquity they'd acquired, pumping him for information on the books he'd agreed to write.

Joshua, another brother whom I'd always been close to, linked his fingers through mine. "I just want two minutes of your time, baby girl. We need to catch up."

Together we climbed the staircase leading to Aunt Estelle's bedroom. It was the only place unoccupied by guests and therefore a good place to talk.

Fingers intertwined, we sat on the bed facing each other.

"How's Leslie?" I asked, referring to his fiancée.

"Wonderful. Perfect. She worries about you. Anything new on your end?" Josh asked.

"Nothing exciting. I'm just getting back into the swing of things after coming back from Tibet."

"Sorry things didn't work out the way you expected. Wasn't the plan for you to be gone several months?"

"Yes, I got tossed a bone, though. I was given the job of repairing Bhaisajyaguru. It took less time than expected, and I still got my bonus. The Chinese government was very embarrassed as you might guess. The Minister of External Affairs was forced to write a public apology to the United States and a personal apology to our father. It all worked out in the end."

Joshua's fingers squeezed mine. "From what I read it was a real mess. Who would expect top government officials to misappropriate funds? Those monies, a result of grants, were designated to conserve and preserve antiquities. They were not to be funneled into some greedy person's pockets to support some bureaucrat's high standard of living. Plus, you could have been killed."

Josh had no tolerance or patience for unethical behavior. He sounded outraged. We were very similar in that regard. But I was over my anger now. I'd gotten what I wanted—my father's name was cleared and I'd been paid enough to get him better medical attention, plus I'd added a little something extra to my bank account.

"How's your love life?" Joshua asked, smoothly changing the conversation.

"What love life?"

"Uh, I thought I'd heard something about you and Damon getting back together."

I felt my cheeks heat up. "You heard wrong." I was practically snapping his head off. I hadn't heard word one from Damon since returning home and I felt hurt and snubbed. "I needed an X-ray infared technologist to accompany me to Tibet," I went on to explain, softening my tone. "Damon's salary was reasonable so I hired him."

"Interesting."

"What's that supposed to mean?"

Before Josh could respond there was a knock at the door. Matthew, my middle brother, stuck his head in through a crack. He wore a smile as wide as the proverbial Cheshire cat. "Sorry to interrupt, children, but one of our guests is asking for Phoenix."

"We're pretty much done anyway." I hopped off the bed. "We'll talk about this later," I said, preceding Josh out.

When I got to the hallway I could tell the noise level, fueled by alcohol, had risen. I assumed that a friend of our dad's, someone who probably had not seen me in years, was inquiring about my whereabouts. I'd been inundated with questions about Tibet. Everyone wanted to know the sordid details about the crooked operation I'd uncovered.

A few were intrigued to hear what living in Lhasa was really like.

Following Matthew, and with Josh trailing me, I pushed my way into the dining room where people were already working their way through dessert, coffee and after-dinner drinks.

I turned to Matthew. "Where is this person?"

"Right behind you, Phe."

I went still. *He* was the last person I'd expected to see my father's party. "Damon, what are you doing here?"

"Your brothers invited me. I came to say congratulations to your dad and I wanted to see you." He took a sip of the drink in his hand.

I'd been home for almost a month and he hadn't thought to contact me before now? I'd become mostly okay with that, figuring our business was done. There was always the off chance I might run into him on another project. I'd deal with it then. Our little fling was over.

I wanted to murder my brothers for putting me in such an uncomfortable situation. They knew exactly what had transpired between us ages ago. Back then they'd threatened to dismember Damon limb by limb. I guess now all had been forgiven. They'd assumed since we'd gone to Tibet together we were friends.

And while the Damon I'd been with in Tibet

was an entirely different person than the one in Florence, he still had an arrogant, macho streak that no amount of enlightenment would fully cure.

"Where can we go to talk, Phe?" Damon asked, taking my arm.

I thought about it. Aunt Estelle's bedroom was not an option, certainly not one for Damon and me. Outside, remnants of the first snow that had fallen in New York coated the brick terrace off the kitchen. I took him there.

Damon and I stood awkwardly facing each other. I stood huddled into the hood of my sweatshirt, my hands stuffed in the bulky pockets, my breath coming in gigantic white puffs. Damon acted as if thirty-degree weather was no big deal.

"You wanted to talk," I snarled. "So talk."

"You're not very gracious, Phe."

Graciousness had nothing to do with it. I hated myself for still being attracted to him.

"I haven't been in touch because I needed space," Damon admitted. "I needed some time to think."

A huge admission on his part and one I didn't dare interpret. I held breath. "What are you trying to say?"

Damon's long fingers curled around my wrist. His smoky eyes looked into mine and I couldn't look away.

"I've been offered a job in the Caribbean," he tempted me. "It's a six-week assignment in Dominica. I'd like you to come along. Will you?"

I couldn't believe it. Damon asking me as a team. Finally.

"I need a restorer, Phe, to work alongside me. Think aquamarine oceans, blue skies overhead. There's been an excavation of Carib and Arawak implements. I've been commissioned to authenticate them. It wouldn't be all work. We could take a side trip to explore other islands and maybe even climb a volcano or two."

I was flattered. Bowled over.

"Think, Phe, a chance to work together again, a chance to really get to know each other. I'd really like you to come."

It took me half a minute to think about it.

I let a beat or two go by before saying, "Only if you tell me what the job's going to pay."

"It will pay with my commitment to your career. I truly respect the lengths you went to clear your dad's name, Phe."

"My job and my dad are very important to me."

"I'm hoping I can be, too. Admit it, Phe. We can make a great team."

I knew it. And soon I'd tell him so.

I came in close and put my arms around his neck. "When do we leave?"

DON'T MISS
THIS SEXY NEW SERIES
FROM KIMANI ROMANCE!

THE BRADDOCKS

SECRET SON

*Power, passion and politics
are all in the family.*

HER LOVER'S LEGACY by Adrianne Byrd
August 2008

SEX AND THE SINGLE BRADDOCK
by Robyn Amos
September 2008

SECOND CHANCE, BABY by A.C. Arthur
October 2008

THE OBJECT OF HIS PROTECTION
by Brenda Jackson
November 2008

www.kimanipress.com

KPBSS0808

Just one look was all it took....

always a
KNIGHT

Book #3 in The Knight Family trilogy

Bestselling Author
WAYNE JORDAN

Aspiring songstress Tori Matthews stirs such
passion in Russell Knight, she's just the girl to change
his playboy ways. But as things begin to heat up
between them, Tori is forced to choose between their
growing passion and a shot at stardom.

"Jordan weaves an unbelievably romantic story
with enough twists and turns to keep any reader
enthralled until the very end."
—*Romantic Times BOOKreviews*
on ONE GENTLE KNIGHT

Available the first week of August wherever books are sold.

KIMANI
ROMANCE

When lightning strikes,
there's no holding back...

NATIONAL BESTSELLING AUTHOR

ROCHELLE ALERS

Taken by Storm

Book #3 of The Whitfield Brides trilogy

When Marshal Raphael Madison becomes
Simone Whitfield's live-in bodyguard during a
high-profile trial, Simone finds his presence stirs up a
storm of longing. Soon their electrifying closeness leads
to an endless night of uncontrollable passion. But will the
morning after bring regrets…or promises of forever?

Meet the Whitfields of New York—experts at coordinating
other people's weddings, but not so great at arranging
their own love lives.

Available the first week of August, wherever books are sold.

ARABESQUE®

www.kimanipress.com

KPRAI100808

Dark, rich and delicious…how could she resist?

NATIONAL BESTSELLING AUTHOR

ROCHELLE ALERS

The Sweetest Temptation

Book #2 of The Whitfield Brides trilogy

Faith Whitfield's been too busy satisfying the sweet tooth of others
to lament her own love life. But when Ethan McMillan comes
to her rescue, he finds himself falling for the luscious pastry
chef…and soon their passions heat to the boiling point!

Meet the Whitfields of New York—experts at
coordinating other people's weddings, but not so great
at arranging their own love lives.

Available the first week of July wherever books are sold.

ARABESQUE®

NATIONAL BESTSELLING AUTHOR

ROCHELLE ALERS

invites you to meet the Whitfields of New York....

Tessa, Faith and Simone Whitfield know all about coordinating
other people's weddings, and not so much about arranging
their own love lives. But in the space of one unforgettable year,
all three will meet intriguing men who just might bring them their
very own happily ever after....

Long Time Coming

June 2008

The Sweetest Temptation

July 2008

Taken by Storm

August 2008

ARABESQUE®

www.kimanipress.com